CU00704713

What's It All About, Geordie?

Renaissance Man Cometh

Simon Northouse

Flabbergasted Publishing

Copyright © 2022 by Simon Northouse

All rights reserved. This book or parts thereof may not be reproduced in any form, distributed, stored in any retrieval system, or transmitted in any form by any means—electronic, mechanical, photocopy, recording, or otherwise—without prior written permission of the Author, except in the case of brief quotations embodied in critical reviews and certain other non-commercial uses permitted by copyright law.

Disclaimer: This is a work of fiction. Names, characters, businesses, places, events, locales, and incidents are either the products of the author's imagination or used in a fictitious manner. Any resemblance to actual persons, living or dead, or actual events is purely coincidental.

Published by Flabbergasted Publishing

Second Edition

Kindle e-book ISBN-13: 978-0-6452904-5-5

Paperback ISBN-13: 978-0-6489684-3-6

Contents

Chapter One

Birthday Blues

A rapid, high-pitched bleeping cuts through the cacophony of screeching and shouting.

'Geordie! Geordie!' Jackie yells. 'That's the buzzer for the sausage rolls. Take them out of the oven and place them on the counter to cool down, then put in the tray of party pies.'

'I'm busy blowing up balloons. Can't you take them out?' I shout.

'No! I'm about to do some games with the kids outside. Make sure you put the sausage rolls on a board to protect the countertop. And Geordie?'

'What the hell now?' I mutter under my breath. 'Yes, my sweetness and light?'

'Don't forget to collect the cake. You can pick it up from the bakery after two-thirty. Be careful with it. You know how clumsy you can be.'

'Yes, darling, whatever you say, my sweetheart.' I'll shove a broomstick up my arse and sweep the floor at the same time,' I murmur.

I glance over at Mavis, the mother-in-law who has done sweet F.A. since she arrived. Actually, that's not entirely true. She has knocked back the best part of a full bottle of expensive champagne. Not a bad effort for someone who reckons they're on their last legs and has more ailments than a leper in a virus testing laboratory.

'Oh, and Geordie, remember, the oven gloves have a hole in them. Don't burn yourself!'

There are a multitude of seven-year-olds running all over the place like a plague of mice. Worse than them are their mothers and fathers. Why did she invite parents to a seven-year-old's birthday party? When I was a kid, the parents were more than happy to drop their brats off and get a couple of hour's respite. Not these days. It's as much about impressing the adults as it is the children.

I turn the kitchen timer off, don the oven gloves, and carefully pull the tray of sausage rolls from the oven.

'Geordie, do you ever play the market?'

Great! It's Roger, the most boring person I've ever had the misfortune to speak to—and that's saying something. He's been following me around like a lost puppy since he arrived. He's not much older than me but looks about sixty. Short, overweight, balding, sweat stains under the armpits of his blue business shirt.

'I cannae say I do. It's simply another form of gambling. I used to like a wee flutter on the horses twice a week. Not much, a tenner here, a tenner there. But Jackie didn't approve. Said she doesn't believe in gambling. I told her I don't believe in God, but I don't go around telling people to burn their Bibles. Anyway, my little avenue of joy soon got bricked up.'

Roger laughs, the sort of laugh you make when you don't really get the joke. I place the tray down on the countertop and make my way to the fridge.

'Stocks and shares are not really gambling,' Roger continues, oblivious to the fact I find him about as interesting as stale bread. 'It's about keeping abreast of current affairs, reading the tea leaves and sticking your nose in the air and seeing what's adrift at sea.'

The guy has a severe case of the mixed metaphors.

'Aye, is that so?' I reply in a cheery tone which masks my stressed inner turmoil. I pull the tray of party pies from the fridge and head back to the oven. A young boy runs up to me with a three-foot inflatable hammer.

'Hey, Mr Kincaid?' he bellows.

'Aye lad, what is it?' I say, smiling as best I can. He whacks me in the cobblers with the damn thing, breaks out into fits of laughter, then turns and scoots out through the glass doors into the garden. I bend double, not in pain, but in expected pain which doesn't materialise.

'Ha-ha,' Roger snorts. 'Aren't children adorable at this age?'

I right myself and give him a steely gaze. 'Yes, you just want to smother them, don't you?'

'As I was saying, a man in your position, a successful rock star, a music biz celeb, I'm sure you're not short of a bob or two.'

'We get by.'

'Have you done any future planning or thought about the tax breaks? You need to consider your children's future. Do you want them to go through the same financial struggles and poverty you had to endure before you became a success again?'

'And what do you know about my poverty or my struggles?' I ask him suspiciously as I slide the tray into the oven.

He's surprised by the question. 'My wife Cassandra, and Jackie are good chums. She's told Cassandra everything. I probably know you better than yourself.'

'I doubt it, pal.'

Mavis slowly totters towards me. 'Geordie, we seem to be out of champagne. Could you fetch another bottle, please?' she asks.

'It's in the spare fridge in the walk-in-pantry. Be my guest.'

'I'm not as stable on my feet as I used to be. My ankles have swollen up something chronic today. It must be the warm weather.'

You're not stable on your feet because you're half sozzled.

'Excuse me for a moment, Roger, I must replenish supplies.' Every cloud has a silver lining.

Inside the pantry I pull a bottle of champagne from the fridge and grab a chilled bottle of beer. I twist the cap off, slump against the wall, let out a deep sigh, and take three big swigs.

'Oh yes! Nectar,' I murmur. All I need now is a nice spliff, but there's no chance of that. I check my watch. 2:25 pm—only another three hours and thirty-five minutes to go.

It's Wallace, my eldest son's seventh birthday. I'm sure he'd have been just as happy with a few close friends, or maybe a party with his proper family, all the lads and lasses from the band. But no, Jackie had other ideas. I take another glug from the bottle.

'Geordie! Geordie!' The dulcet tones of my wife ring out.

She has three levels in her decibel range. Number three: her soft voice, which is employed most of the time. Number two: her hectoring voice she uses to order me and the boys around which to be fair—we bloody need. And number-one—her battle charge, as if in a chariot facing up to the Roman Legions. Her present call is at number two. The door opens, and she walks in.

'Why are you hiding in here? What are you doing with that beer? Why aren't you in the kitchen? Did you put the buzzer on for the pies?'

I finish the dregs of my bottle and drop it into the bin. 'Just catching a few seconds peace and fetching another bottle of champagne for your alcoholic mother.'

'She's not an alcoholic, she has a lot of issues.'

'Aye, tell me about it... no, don't bother. I've heard it from her a thousand times before.'

'I hope that's your first beer. Have no more until the party's over. You still need to pick the cake up and I need you to be on the ball.'

I stand and grab the bottle of champers. 'Jackie, why did you invite the whole bloody class *and* their parents? When I was a bairn, we could invite three, maybe four, of our best mates at most. The party would last an hour. A few games in the back room, a birthday tea followed by the cake. We would all sing happy birthday, blow out the candles, then everyone would sod off home.'

She turns to leave. 'Things have changed. We understand the world a lot better now. You cannot invite a few close friends from your class these days. Have you not heard of inclusivity? If you exclude some children, you create a barrier, a tier system of who is cool and who is not. It leads to cliques, gangs, and aggression, which permeate throughout life. We are all equal and everyone should be invited. Imagine if it was Wallace or Bobby who didn't receive the birthday invite? Imagine their little broken hearts at being excluded... hmm?'

'I'd tell them to get over it. Big deal. Life isn't like that. All you're doing is creating a false sense of reality for them. Life is tough and cruel, and they need to learn how to roll with it and take the punches.'

She shakes her head in dismay and huffs. 'For God's sake, Geordie, do I have to drag you kicking and screaming into the twenty-first century? Please, try your best... for me?'

She moves towards me, drapes her arms around my neck and kisses me sweetly on the forehead.

I melt and let out a sigh. 'Aye, okay... scouts' honour. But I'm warning you; once this is over and we've got the wee ones to bed, I'm not sitting on the couch all night watching Crimewatch with your mother. She looks like most of the photofits they splash up on the screen, anyway.'

I get a rare laugh. 'Okay, deal. We'll get an early night. I'm feeling quite frisky actually, so you may be in luck.' She opens the door to leave. 'Oh and watch your language... you're in refined company now, you're not with the band! And don't forget the party pies!'

I stick my head out of the pantry door and scan the room. I'm safe. Roger is speaking to a woman whose expression looks like she's got a cactus stuck up her backside. Completely understandable, when in conversation with Roger. She fumbles about in her handbag, probably searching for a bottle of Valium or a gun.

I slink back into the room. The noise is deafening! Bloody hard floors. I wanted carpet; Jackie wanted tiles—we got tiles. I decide to put some music on to lighten proceedings. The kids won't give a damn, but the parents might appreciate the sweet dulcet tones of Sam Cooke.

Ah, yes, that's better.

I pull the cork from the bottle of champers and place it on the countertop. Within seconds, Mavis materialises like a wasp to a honeypot.

'Geordie! You're such a good lad!' she says as she pats me on the shoulder, grabs the bottle, and disappears into the throng. I glance out of the window and notice the uncontrolled brat, with the inflatable hammer, is smashing the shit out of Wallace. My blood boils!

Let it be, Geordie.

Donning the oven mitts I return to my duties. As I'm checking the party pies, a finger gently jabs me in the ribs.

'Hey big boy, how's it going?'

I recognise the prod, the voice. It's Sandra, another alcoholic. This one is lecherous and a bit of a dippy hippy, to boot.

'Hi, Sandra. Yep, all good. What about you?' I reply.

'Very noisy in here, what with the adults, kids, and music... don't you think?' I don't have time to answer. 'Last year I did a summer school course in Feng Shui. You should try it sometime.'

I glance at the timer. 'I'm not really into martial arts. Give me boxing any day of the week.'

She laughs and slaps me playfully on the shoulder. 'Oh, you're such a wag! I also did a course in Nuru massage. It's an erotic Japanese technique from Kawasaki. Have you ever tried it out?'

'No, can't say I have. Although, I did once test ride a Yamaha XT-500,' I reply, reluctantly turning to gaze at her.

'Do you ever take anything seriously?'

'I try not to. There's far too much seriousness in the world for my liking. If everyone would slow down a bit, and chill, the world would be a far better place.'

'Nuru—it's body-to-body massage, all oiled up. It's very sensual,' she persists. 'We also spent an hour on learning the intricacies of prostate massage.'

'Sounds like fun.'

She moves closer and stares into my eyes. 'You look like a man who has an irritated prostate. Have you thought about getting it massaged?'

'Not recently. Although, I've reached the age now where my doctor, Hamish McDougall, likes to give it a poke once a year. I cannae say I've taken to the practice with open arms. His fingers are the size of Lebanese cucumbers.'

She picks fluff off my shirt. 'If you'd like a slim, lady finger to give it a go, I'm always available,' she says, sporting a lascivious grin.

'Thanks for the offer. I'll bear it in mind.'

'Geordie! Geordie!' Jackie yells. 'Have the sausage rolls cooled down yet? We need to feed these children.'

I place my hand around a roll to test the heat. 'Yep, they're good to go,' I reply.

Sandra moves behind me, places her hands on my shoulders and kneads at my flesh. Jackie appears and glares at me. I shrug.

'Don't mind me, Jackie,' Sandra begins. 'I'm trying to relax your husband. He's very tense. His aura is a pale blue, never a good sign, and he has an irritated prostate. I offered to massage it for him, but he seems a little reticent. Men are so squeamish about these things, don't you find?'

Jackie sidles up to her and whispers in her ear. 'If anyone is going to massage his prostate, it will be me, his wife. Now get your hands off my husband!' she hisses.

The massage abruptly stops. 'I was only trying to help.'

'Oh, I know what you were trying to do.'

'Ladies, please,' I intervene. 'No one is going to massage anyone's prostate, well apart from Hamish McDougall. Now, can you please retreat to your corners and act civil? Jackie, the rolls are ready to go. Another five minutes and the party pies will be done. You take care of the outside; I'll take care of the inside.'

Jackie grabs the tray of sausage rolls and departs.

'I'm not sure what her problem is?' Sandra sniffs as she grabs a glass of champagne and throws it back like water.

Why do parents think a kid's birthday party is a good place to get hammered? I put the mitts on and head to the oven. Sandra is back... hovering.

'How's life in the pop business?' she asks.

'Pop business?'

'Yes. Sex, drugs, and rock and roll.'

'It's going swimmingly. Last album is still selling well. We had a successful mini-tour a few months back, and me and Bill are working on some new songs.'

'Have you ever met Pink?'

'No.'

'Lady Gaga?'

'No.'

'What about Katy Perry?'

'Erm... no.'

'Have you met *anyone* famous?'

'Yeah, loads of people. Rod Stewart, for one.'

'Really? And how did you find him?'

'I turned left into the toilets as he was coming out. I don't mean *coming out*, I meant leaving.'

'What is he like as a person?'

'Very nice. Can't fault the bloke. Very short though,' I explain.

Her hand slips onto my groin. 'I bet everyone's short compared to you,' she says, sporting a lustful, slightly drunken leer.

Christ!

I gently take her hand and remove it.

'Stand back, these pies are about done.'

As I extract the pies, I throw a quick glance outside at the dozens of kids running around like maniacs. The hammer bully boy is running full pelt across the garden and deliberately rams into Wallace, sending him flying to the ground. He picks himself up and brushes himself off.

The little shit! Someone needs to have a word.

'Sandra, who's the little shitehawk with the inflatable hammer?'

She gazes out the window with drowsy eyes.

'Cohen Asher. He's Madeline's little boy.'

'Madeline?'

'Madeline Asher,' she says, nodding towards the woman with the pained expression who's enduring Roger. 'She's president of the Parents and Teachers Association. I'd keep on the right side of her. She's a super bitch and a virtue signaller.'

'A virtue signaller, what the hell's that?'

She giggles. 'It's someone who deliberately shows *contempt* or *support* for political ideals or cultural mores. In the old days, people called it token gestures. Similar to super-rich pop stars sitting in their palatial mansions banging on about saving the planet.'

'Is that a dig?' I say.

'Not really. I have all your CDs. At least when you talk about the planet, you shine a light on your own hypocrisy. I know everything about you and your band mates. Robbo is an alcohol dependent dope fiend. Flaky is a pescatarian, God fearing, pain in the arse. Will Harding is a moody control freak. And...'

'And me?'

'You... hmm. You are...' she pauses. 'It doesn't matter.' She turns to leave. I'm intrigued and grab her gently on the shoulder and spin her around.

'Go on. You've insulted my three best friends. You may as well go the whole hog.'

She takes another gulp of champagne as she flutters her eyelashes at me. 'Troubled. Quick to anger. You have issues... long seated issues. You're a good man who sometimes makes poor decisions.'

I consider her assessments for a moment. She's mainly correct, at least at face value.

'You're probably right about me, but not about my mates. All you see is the 2D version, the cardboard cut-outs, newspaper headlines, soundbites. You don't know the actual people behind those public images.

Believe it or not, there's a lot of love between us, not that we ever acknowledge it. We also have a moral compass... when to do the right thing. We admit our mistakes, and we know how to swallow our pride and forgive, even Flaky and Bill.

Anyway, back to Madeline Asher. According to you, she's a virtue signaller who is head of the PTA. What else?'

'She's passive aggressive, a gas-lighter, and a master of white-anting... and she's exceptionally good at what she does.'

'You've obviously had a run in with her?'

'Once or twice.'

'Over what?'

'I'm a single parent. I struggle financially. Madeline respects money, not people. It's why she's here today. This will be a great honour for her. Being invited to the birthday party of the son of a rock star is something she can brag about at her exclusive dinner parties. It's all about perception with her. She likes to come over as the well-to-do conservative go-getter, but she also wants to appear cool. Like I said, her public persona is everything. She has to be in control, in the spotlight.'

'And her husband?'

'A banker in London. Hardly ever home.'

'I see. Well, that lad of hers is out of control and someone needs to speak to him.'

'Don't say a word about Cohen! He's her golden boy who can do no wrong. She thinks he'll become a future leader.'

'Of what?'

'The Conservative Party, then Prime Minister.'

'Christ! Give me strength. The lad's seven years old. Maybe when he grows up, he'll become a bricklayer or joiner, you know, something worthwhile.'

'You don't know Madeline. Once she sets her mind to something, it usually happens. She's the one who has been spearheading the vanguard to raise money for a new children's playground at the school. Although, to be honest, she's not made much headway.'

'How much do they need?'

'Fifty thousand... give or take.'

I make my way back to the oven.

Roger collars me. 'As I was saying before, about the market...'

I put the gloves on as Sandra resumes massaging my shoulders.

'Geordie, I don't know what happened to the bottle of champagne. I only had one glass and now it's disappeared,' Mavis starts.

Aye, down your gullet.

I pull the tray of pies out. 'Ah! Fuck it!' I yell, as the skin of my thumb comes into contact with sizzling hot metal.

I involuntary throw the tray into the air as the room falls silent. The pies land with a gloopy splat over the hard, unforgiving tiles.

Chapter Two

Oops! I'll Get My Coat

I ring the bell on the counter. A few seconds later, a ruddy faced chap appears.

'I'm here to collect a birthday cake for Wallace Kincaid. The truck tyre?' I explain.

The guy grins at me. 'Ah yes. I won't be a minute.'

He disappears out the back as I tap at the countertop impatiently. A few seconds pass before he returns. He's gripping one end of a board as a colleague holds the other end. In the middle is a cake of enormous proportions.

'Hell's bells and buckets of blood! I didn't realise it was to scale!' I exclaim.

The guy smiles at me as he makes his way from behind the counter. 'Pretty impressive, eh? If you'd like to open the boot of your car, we can drop it straight in.'

Outside, I open the door of the Range Rover. The guys gently rest the cake in the boot. He fumbles about in his apron and pulls something out.

'Here, these are the candles. They're sparklers. We had them specially made.'

He hands me a metallic object which has about thirty sparklers, cut down, and arranged into the number 7. I place it next to the cake and slam the door shut.

'Right, thanks. Wallace will be as pleased as punch.'

As I make my way to the driver's door, the baker coughs.

'Ahem, Mr Kincaid. You need to pay for it,' he says, almost embarrassed.

'I'm sorry. I thought my wife had already paid. How much do I owe you?' I reply as I pull my wallet out.

'A hundred and twenty for the cake,' he says gleefully.

I feel slightly dizzy. 'A hundred and twenty! It's not a bloody wedding cake! It's a bit of sponge with black icing made to look like the wheel of a truck.' I peel the notes off and hand them to him.

'Oh, and twenty for the candles,' he adds as he slips the money into his apron pocket.

'Jesus H Christ,' I mumble to myself as I hand over more notes.

'Thank you, and I hope the party goes well,' the baker says in a cheery mood as he and his assistant walk back into the shop.

⌁≫≫ ≪≪⌁

I struggle up the stairs, through the front door and into the kitchen with the giant cake and place it on the counter as various parents gather around, admiring the culinary work of art. Jackie makes an appearance.

'Wow!' she exclaims. 'Right, give me two minutes to round up the children, then bring it onto the patio table.' She heads outside with an excited hop and skip.

Roger is back. 'If you want to get together for a few hours one weekend, I could take you through the intricacies of the stock market step-by-step and explain how it works.'

'Thanks Roger, I appreciate it. The thing is Jackie deals with all the finances. But I'll tell you what. Why don't you grab her when the party is over and arrange a date and time with her? I'm sure she'll be thrilled.'

He smiles warmly at me. 'Okay, I will.'

Outside, Jackie doesn't seem to have had much effect on corralling the kids. I pick the cake up and head towards the glass doors.

'Stand back, stand back, man with cake coming through.'

The crowd parts, then drops in behind me as though I'm the Pied Piper.

'Geordie, when you get a minute, could you fetch another bottle of champagne?' Mavis calls out, appearing distinctly sloshed.

Someone pinches me hard on the arse cheeks. I glance over my shoulder as Sandra winks at me. My limited patience is wearing thin. I navigate through the doors onto the concrete patio and spy the brat with the inflatable hammer. He runs up to Wallace and whacks him as hard as he can in the face with the damn thing!

That's it!

I place the cake down on the concrete, leap down the steps, and sprint across the garden.

'Oi, you! You little shite!' I drop to my haunches and jab my finger at him. 'If you bully my son ever again, I'll kick your bloody arse into the middle of next week!' I bellow.

For a split second, he looks horrified before he erupts into screams and tears, turns tail, and runs back towards the house.

Shit! What have I done?

A gigantic wave of embarrassment rolls over me. Every parent is standing on the patio, mouths agape, staring in complete silence at me. Jackie's hands cup her mouth. Madeline has her arms held open as her distraught son rushes into them. Rooted to the spot as if frozen in time, are the other children. I rise gingerly to my feet.

'The lad's a bully. It needs calling out,' I offer weakly as a way of an apology, instantly regretting my words.

'Oh! Damn and blast!'

Everyone slowly turns to gawp at Mavis, who is tottering around with a large clod of birthday cake stuck to her foot.

Chapter Three

Phone A Friend

Jackie ushers the last of the parents and children through the kitchen and out into the hallway.

'Thank you so much for coming. I'm terribly sorry about all the upset. My husband doesn't normally behave that way. He's been under a lot of stress lately,' Jackie apologises.

'We fully understand. We can all reach breaking point sometimes.'

I'm leaning against the kitchen counter, preparing myself for the verbal onslaught which will shortly be underway. I glance around the room. The boys are playing quietly in the corner with a truck and a crane. Mavis is sitting on a lounge chair staring out into the garden. In between sips of white wine, she occasionally sniffs. I hear the front door quietly close. Jackie marches back into the kitchen.

'Wallace!' she shouts. 'There's a large box in the corner. Why don't you collect together all your birthday presents, put them in the box and take them to your room.'

'Okay, mam,' he replies, detecting Jackie's battle cry.

'And Robert, you can help,' she adds.

'Oh mam, do I have to?' he moans, *not* detecting Jackie's battle cry.

'Yes, you do!' she snaps at him.

As the boys gather their toys, Jackie goes to the fridge and pulls out a bottle of white wine. She grabs an exceptionally large glass and fills it to the brim. She takes three large gulps, then gently places the half-empty glass on the counter. Her fingers slowly run over the scorch mark left by the sausage roll tray. The boys shuffle past, each holding one end of the box. As they climb the stairs, Robert sniggers.

'What's so funny?' Wallace asks.

'Grandma, when she stood in your birthday cake,' he replies, chuckling away.

'It wasn't funny,' Wallace says.

'It was.'

'Well, it was a little,' he agrees as he giggles. I tap on the bench with my wedding ring. Jackie is hunched over her wineglass, head down. The occasional sniffle from Mavis is the only sound.

'Well, well, well,' Jackie murmurs.

She tips the rest of the wine down her throat, and refills the glass, depositing the empty bottle into the recycling bin.

She turns to me. 'My God! You've done some stupid, reckless, idiotic things in your time, but this... this! This is the icing on the cake.'

A poor analogy considering the incident with the sponge tyre.

'The boy's a bully. He needed telling,' I mumble, instantly wishing I could keep my big mouth shut sometimes.

Her eyes fire up. 'My God! You really are a moron, aren't you? Do you not see the ridiculous irony in your words? A giant of a man screaming abuse and threatening violence towards a six-year-old boy! A bully picking on a bully! And so the cycle continues!' she screams at me.

Another gulp of wine, sniffs, throws her hair back over her head.

'That's it now; we'll have to change schools. We'll be pariahs, social outcasts. No one will associate with us, and no one will want their child playing with Wallace. I can imagine what the parents will say the next time one of his friends asks if he can play over at the Kincaid's. "Sorry son, but his father is an aggressive, unhinged buffoon. Best you don't play with Wallace anymore." I'm expecting a knock on the door any moment from the police. They could arrest you over this.'

'You're overreacting,' I whisper.

'Overreacting! Overreacting! No, I'll tell you what overreacting is; threatening to kick a six-year-old's arse into the middle of next week—now that's an overreaction! And it was only the start of it. Not content with emotionally scarring a little boy for life, you proceed to insult everyone else.'

'It wasn't everyone. Only a few select people.'

'You told Roger you'd had more stimulating conversations with a bowl of cauliflower soup, then told him to piss off! You called Sandra a saggy breasted old trollop and if you wanted a rub-and-tug, you'd go to the knocking shop at the end of town where the women are a damn sight younger and don't apply their make-up with a plastering trowel. Oh, and let's not forget about my mother. What was it you called her? Ah yes, a neurotic, drunken, old witch!'

'Harridan,' I correct.

'Sorry?' she snaps.

'I called her a neurotic, drunken, old harridan. I didn't call her a witch.'

'Oh, that's okay, then. Did you hear that, mother? Geordie doesn't think you're a witch after all, just a harridan.'

Mavis snuffles as she stoically gazes out of the window with teary eyes. Jackie pats the countertop gently with her palm.

'I'm not even going to mention the birthday cake, party pies, the scorch mark, or the fact you completely ruined your son's seventh birthday.'

I think she just has. But best let it go.

'He won't forget this one in a hurry, if ever.' There's silence for a moment before she starts up again. 'I really thought we were making progress. I really did. But it's one step forward and two steps back with you, Geordie. I'm not sure what to do. I'm not sure we have a future together.'

She lets out a deep sigh as I spot a couple of tears drip down her cheek. I move towards her.

'Jackie, I'm sorry, I truly am.' I reach out to dry her tears, but she slaps my hand away.

'Don't... just don't!' she barks at me. 'You're always sorry. How many times have I heard it before? It doesn't stop you doing stupid things again... does it?'

'I don't mean to do them. They just seem to happen.'

'No!' she screeches in my face. 'They don't just happen! You *let* them happen!'

She puts the glass to her lips, throws the wine back, then wipes her cheeks on the back of her hands.

'Right, let's tidy this mess up,' she states matter-of-factly surveying the detritus of wasted food, paper plates, balloons, and birthday cake which smear the tiles. 'Then I'm going to bed.'

⇢⇢⇠⇠

After two hours and not a single word uttered between us, the place is back to normal. All clean and tickety-boo.

'Come along, mother. It's time for bed.'

Mavis, who for a moment I thought was suffering from rigor mortis, rises wearily to her feet.

'Yes, dear,' is her only response.

Jackie takes her mother's arm, and they shuffle out of the kitchen towards the stairs.

'I don't care where you sleep,' Jackie says, 'but you're not sleeping with me,' is her parting shot.

They disappear from view as their footsteps plod up the stairs. I pull a tumbler from the cupboard and fill it to the top with scotch and knock it back in two thirsty gulps. Clutching a chilled beer, I head into the back garden and deposit two bin bags of recycling into the wheelie bin before entering my shed. Standing on tiptoes, I retrieve the little tin box from the top of a shelf and pull out a joint. In the garden I sit on the bottom step and spark up. As I swig beer and inhale smoke, I relax for the first time since I stepped out of bed this morning.

'Well done, Geordie... well done. Another fuck-up of gargantuan proportions,' I mumble. I pull my phone from my pocket and tap on Billy Boy's annoyed looking image. It rings.

'Hey Geordie, how's it going?'

'Are you busy?'

'No. The kids are in bed, and Fiona's in the house watching some shite reality TV show. I'm in the studio laying down some backing tracks for a couple of new songs I'm working on. They sound amazing. How's the birthday boy, hope it all went well? Fiona told me Jackie was organising a massive party for him. I bet you enjoyed that... ha-ha!'

I take another toke on the joint and gaze up at the shimmering night sky.

'Ahem, it didn't go too well actually. I threatened a kid who was bullying Wallace, insulted several guests, dropped party pies on the floor, burnt the bench top and called the mother-in-law a neurotic, drunken, old harridan.'

'Another day in the life of Geordie Kincaid. Nothing new,' he chuckles.

'It's not funny, Bill. It's serious.'

'Had you been on the whisky?'

'No. I only had one solitary bottle of beer. I lost it. The red mist came down.'

'Geordie, that temper of yours... you need to get help. I've been telling you for years.'

'I know. If only I'd listened and acted sooner.'

'It's never too late. Get some counselling. See a psychologist or something. Find out what causes you to explode.'

'It's when I see people doing the wrong thing. It makes my blood boil.'

'I understand, but there are better ways to put the world to rights than lashing out. You're an intelligent man, sort of. Use words, not threats, to solve problems.'

'Aye. Easy to say.'

'How's Jackie?'

'How do you think?'

'Hmm... I can imagine.'

'By her own standards, she was quite restrained. In fact, it unnerved me.'

'What stage are you at now? The silent treatment?'

'Aye. And sleeping alone. She's not sure about our relationship anymore. I'm worried, Bill. I think I might have fucked it up for good this time.'

'Geordie, don't stress. It's another storm, and all storms pass. They don't last forever.'

'I'm not so sure. She was almost fatalistic. What can I do, Bill? How can I put it right?'

'Listen to me. I get this off Fiona from time to time. What you've got to do is tuck your tail between your legs, pull your head in, and keep your big gob shut. Ride it out. Tomorrow, get on the phone and call all the people you insulted and offer your sincerest apologies. Make some bullshit up about stress or something. Then ring around everyone else who was at the party and apologise to them as well. After a few days, do something nice together as a family. A day out or go to a restaurant, or the cinema, something where you can bond together. And don't rise to any bait she dangles in front of you. She'll niggle away, making sarcastic and caustic comments. Suck them up, they're only words. They can't hurt you if you don't let them.'

I sip on my beer, then stub out the joint. 'Cheers Bill, I feel a lot better already, although it could be the weed.'

'No worries, pal. Hey, when are you down next? Is it this week or next?'

'Week on Wednesday. I've got the bass parts worked out for three of the songs. I still need some inspiration for the fourth. Right, I best go. I need to make myself a bed up on the sofa.'

'Ha-ha! I've been there, brother—I've been there.'

'Cheers, buddy. Take care.'

'You too, Geordie. Oh, and tell Wallace his Uncle Billy hopes he had a very special, even memorable, birthday and I have a present waiting for him.'

'Aye, okay.'

I walk back inside and pour myself a shot of whisky. Three loud raps on the front door give me a start. I glance at the clock—8:40 pm. I walk into the hallway and pull open the door. Stood on the top step are Dougie Constable and Trevor Dankworth, my occasional drinking buddies and darts partners. They're dressed in their uniforms—police uniforms.

'Hi Dougie, Trevor,' I nod at them. 'What can I do for you?' I ask, already knowing the answer.

Trevor nods back and smiles. 'Geordie,' he says, receiving a stern glance from Dougie.

Trevor drops his head and looks sheepish as Dougie pulls his notebook from his pocket.

'Ahem,' he clears his throat. 'Are you Mr Allan Kincaid, A.K.A. Geordie Kincaid, of No. 3 Cumberland Place, Edinburgh?' he quizzes in an authoritarian voice.

'A.K.A. stands for, also known as,' Trevor whispers to me.

He receives another withering glance from Dougie. I stare at the street sign across the road—Cumberland Place, then at the number on my door—No. 3.

'Of course I bloody am. You know that. We play darts with each other most Wednesdays at the Lion's Head.'

'I'll take that as a yes, shall I?' Dougie replies as he combs through his notes. 'Do you mind if we come in, sir? I'd prefer to discuss this delicate matter in private.'

'Aye, all right. Come in, boys.' I hold open the door and usher them into the kitchen.

They both take off their peaked caps and place them on the kitchen counter.

'I'm about to have a wee dram. Would you care to join me?' I say as I point at the whisky bottle.

Trevor grins broadly. 'Oh, aye, that would be pure dead brilliant, Geordie.'

Dougie shoots his partner a glare.

'May I remind you, Constable Dankworth, we are still on active duty. There's another eighteen minutes before our shift ends.'

Trevor looks suitably chastised and tilts his head to one side. 'Aye, I suppose you're right, Constable Constable. Better give it a miss, but thanks anyway, Geordie.'

'Suit yourselves,' I reply as I neck the whisky down in one and refill my glass. 'What's all this about, lads?'

'We've had a formal complaint,' Dougie begins, 'from a Madeline Asher. She says at approximately 3:15 pm this afternoon you threatened her son.'

I let out a sigh. 'I didnae threaten him. Okay, I may have yelled at him, but only in anger. I'd never hurt a bairn.'

Dougie eyes me suspiciously while Trevor appears embarrassed he's even here at all.

'Nevertheless,' Dougie continues, 'I am here to have a quiet word. The lady in question doesn't wish to make a formal complaint, but she wants you to know the event has traumatised her son. She says in a civilised society aggressive behaviour and threats of violence must not be tolerated.'

'That's exactly what I was doing—not tolerating aggressive behaviour,' I say, becoming riled with the proceedings. 'Her son is a little shite! He was bullying the other kids. In the old days he'd have copped a quick clip around the ear, and it would have been the end of the matter. I notice his mother was quick to turn a blind eye to her own son's aggressive behaviour.'

'Do you wish to lodge a counter-complaint?' Dougie asks, completely misreading my explanation.

'No! Of course I bloody don't!' I snap. I take a deep breath and calm down. 'Look, I'll tell you what I'll do. I'll call her tomorrow and offer my apologies. I'll sort things out.'

Trevor smiles. 'I think this is a positive outcome for everyone, don't you, Constable Constable?'

Dougie doesn't look convinced and stares at me as he slips his notebook back into his breast pocket.

'Hmm... okay. Let that be the end of the matter and make sure you apologise. I don't want this sort of nonsense on my patch. We've got hardened criminals to catch. I don't want to be wasting my precious time on petty trifles,' Dougie explains as he clasps his hands behind his back and rocks back and forth on his heels.

Christ! Hardened criminals to catch! I've known the dynamic duo for over five years, and they couldn't catch a hardened criminal if they were attending a hardened criminal convention.

Dougie's severe frown eventually melts and a thin wisp of a smile spreads across his face. He glances at the clock.

'About that whisky?' he says.

I pull two tumblers from the cupboard and pour a generous shot of whisky into each one.

Dougie glances at Trevor. 'And not a word to the Sergeant, Constable Dankworth,' he says, tapping the end of his nose.

Trevor grins. 'Of course not, Constable Constable... not a word.'

Chapter Four

Contrition

Three days have elapsed, and Jackie hasn't uttered a single word to me. I did as Bill advised and rang everyone from the party. They all seemed to accept my apology, even Madeline Asher. But one never knows what people really think.

It's Sunday morning and the boys are dressed, fed, and quietly watching TV. The gentle patter of Jackie's bare feet make their way down the stairs. She walks in looking tired, worn out.

'Morning, love. I have your breakfast in the oven, keeping warm. I'll fix you a coffee.'

She doesn't reply but slumps wearily onto a barstool at the kitchen bench. I place the coffee in front of her, then retrieve a large picnic basket from the pantry.

'What's that for?' she says, staring at the hamper.

Progress—she speaks.

'I thought I'd take the boys to the beach this morning. I have a picnic prepared. Chicken legs, egg, and cress sandwiches, lemonade, some packets of crisps and a flask of coffee for us... I mean me. Afterwards, I'll take them to the cinema. They're showing Shaun The Sheep, in town. Wallace has been badgering me to see it for weeks. On the way home I thought I'd take them to McDonald's, as a treat.'

I take her breakfast plate from the oven and place it in front of her. 'It's your favourite; crispy bacon with scrambled eggs and pancakes smothered in maple syrup. Don't know how you can have maple syrup on it, but each to their own.'

'Thanks.' She offers me a weak smile and tucks into the food.

'I'd like it very much if you'd come with us, but I understand if you want to be alone. Anyway, your choice.'

'Yes, I would like to come. We're family, aren't we?' she says.

I try to restrain a giant beam but fail miserably. She's annoyed at first, but slowly a reluctant sliver of a smile melts across her face.

'Aye, we're family—for better or for worse.'

'Hmm... indeed.'

⫸⫷

Wallace and Robert are playing in the shallow breakers. As each wave rolls in they run back up the beach, screaming and laughing. I'm sitting on a picnic blanket with Jackie. It's a warm day, the sea a twinkling bluey green, the gentle breeze refreshing. She's still in sulk mode, so I don't push the situation.

'Sandwich and coffee?' I offer.

'Hmm, yes, thank you.'

I unload the picnic hamper and pass her a sandwich.

'We don't do things like this often enough,' she says as I pour the coffee.

'No, we don't. I'm not sure why. We have plenty of time, not like those other poor sods who have to be at their desks by nine every day. We live an easy life... I mean, I live an easy life. I know how hard you work.'

'It's the little things,' she murmurs wistfully, entranced by the view.

'Sorry?'

'The little things. Like this, spending quality time with the children. Going for walks. Taking them to the park or pool or even simply reading a story to them. It's the little things I'll remember the most... and miss when they're finally gone.'

I hand her the coffee and decide now is as good a time as any. 'Jackie, when can we get back to normal? It's killing me seeing you like this.'

'That depends.'

'On what?'

'On you. Can you change? Do you want to change?'

'Yes and yes.'

She puts her cup down and turns to me. 'Geordie, you've never talked about your early childhood. All I've heard is from Fiona, who got it second-hand from Will. Whenever I try to broach the subject, you shut me down.'

I sigh and shuffle uneasily on the picnic blanket.

'I cannae remember much about it. Only the day...' I stop as the nightmare plays out in my head.

'The day your brother was killed?' she whispers as she strokes my cheek.

'Ahem, aye,' I mumble.

'You were coming back from the cinema, and he got knocked down by a car?'

'Yep.'

'How old were you both?'

I stare at my two weans, who are splashing each other in the shallow waves.

'A little younger than our two,' I say, nodding towards the boys. 'I was six and Iain was four.'

'I'm so sorry.'

'It's a long time ago now, but it's still raw. It's not just the loss, it's... it's...' I tail off.

'Go on?'

'It's the guilt.'

'You don't blame yourself for what happened, surely?'

'I do. I was the older brother. I should have looked out for him... Iain. I wonder what he'd look like now?'

'You were six. A year younger than Wallace. You weren't responsible. Look at him, he's a little innocent boy. He can't be responsible for anyone at his age, not even himself.'

'Aye, I know. I've told myself that a million times, but it doesn't change how I feel. Logic doesn't work.'

'Geordie, I think you need to see someone, a psychiatrist, or psychologist. You need to get these feelings out. They're like a cancer. There is possibly a link between your outburst of anger and your guilt.'

I nod and sip on my coffee.

'If we want to move forward, then you must see someone. Please, do it for me and the boys.'

I gaze into her glassy emerald eyes.

'Aye, you're right. It's something I should have done years ago. I've been a coward. I fear what else might be dug up.'

'Things about your mother and father?'

I laugh. 'About my ma, yes. I didn't have a father.'

'Everyone has a father, even if they're estranged.'

'Not me. Right, I'll get onto it next week.'

'Promise?'

'Cross my heart and hope to die.'

She smiles sweetly at me. 'Good. Right, one more thing,' she begins.

'You're really milking this, aren't you?' I say with a chuckle.

'I want you to ring around all the people you insulted at the party and apologise.'

I stand up and brush sand from my trousers. 'Already done, my little cherub.'

She looks astounded. 'No! When?'

'The day after the party. I rang every single person who attended and apologised... profusely.'

'How did they react? What did you say?'

'Everyone was very understanding. I told Madeline the band would donate a generous amount of money for the new children's playground at the school. She was effusive in her thanks. I also told her I suffered from PTSD after my time serving Queen and Country in the Parachute Regiment. She was almost crying when I eventually hung up.'

'Oh my God! You lied to her! She can look you up on Wikipedia and check your history.'

'I thought of that. I told her I served my time before I joined the band and there's nothing on the public record about it because I was involved in covert operations. You know, my identity needs to be kept secret for security reasons. No doubt every parent at the school will hear about it eventually.'

Jackie jumps to her feet and slaps me playfully on the arm. 'You are unbelievable! And what did Roger and Sandra have to say?'

'You know Roger, insulting him was like insulting a brick. He just started banging on about blue chip shares for fifteen minutes, which, considering the circumstances, I painfully listened to. And Sandra said she could tell I wasn't right because my aura was a pale blue. She's offered to help repair it with reiki and the laying on of hot stones—mad old hippy.'

'I'm not letting her anywhere near you, especially alone. I've got to say I'm impressed. I know how pig-headed you can be, so it must have been very difficult for you to swallow your pride and admit you were in the wrong.'

She moves towards me and puckers up her lips.

'Da! Da! Come quick, Robert's fallen in the water!' Wallace screams.

'Oh shit!' I yell, as I sprint off across the beach.

Chapter Five

Band Meeting

I'm making myself a brew in the kitchen as Jackie fiddles with the laptop in the living room.

'Hurry up, Geordie, we're about to start!' she shouts.

As I saunter into the room, I hear her chatting with the others online. It's the monthly band meeting, this time via video conferencing, something I'm not enamoured with. I hand Jackie her tea, pull up a chair and sit beside her.

'I preferred it when we all met face to face,' I grumble. 'It's not the same speaking to people via a camera on a laptop. It's impersonal. Bloody technology.'

Jackie sips her drink. 'Stop complaining, you Luddite. With young kids, it's not always workable to drop everything and run off to Yorkshire. And it's a long trip.'

'It's only three hours, four if we take the scenic route. It's a pleasant drive.'

'What's he complaining about now?' Fiona asks, laughing on screen.

'He doesn't enjoy having these meetings via laptop. You know what he's like with technology; he still uses an abacus to work out the electricity bill!'

There're guffaws from Fiona, Gillian, and Julie as their faces all line up next to each other on the screen.

'Most amusing. You missed your vocation, dearest,' I moan.

'Where's Will, Robbo and Flaky?' she asks.

'He's coming,' all three women say, talking over each other.

'See what I mean? There are no visual cues. You need body language to have a meaningful conversation.'

The faces of my bandmates appear next to their wives as they take their positions.

'Okay, we're waiting on John Peterson. Ah! Here he is now. Morning, John,' Jackie says as another couple of minutes are wasted as everyone greets one another again.

'Get on with it, woman,' I whisper.

She slaps me on the thigh. 'Right, I'll begin. We'll follow the usual routine and discuss the accounts, website, social media, mailing list, marketing and what's planned for the next twelve months. Please save questions not related to the topic on hand until the end.'

These meetings began over a decade ago when the band decided they would be the masters of their own destiny. No more record companies or publishers. No expensive marketing corporations and advertising agencies or managers taking twenty per cent. No more deadlines built around the eighteen month cycle of album, promotion, tour. And best of all, no more clueless record execs telling us what sort of music to make.

It was fun and liberating at first. There were just the four of us. We would convene at Bill's house once a month and sit around the dining room table and munch on roast beef sandwiches washed down with copious amounts of ice-cold lager. Occasionally, John Peterson, our legal eagle, would take part. Not only did he help us set up the cooperative on a sound legal basis, but his razor-sharp mind also came up with new ideas and better ways to achieve things.

To be honest, looking back, I'm amazed we achieved as much as we did because none of us really had a clue what we were doing. Then our wives and spouses arrived on the scene. Jackie to run the website and mailing list. Gillian to manage the accounts. Julie, the artwork, and Fiona, everything else from replying to fan mail to posting out merchandise. They do a fantastic job; way better than we ever did. If it wasn't for the fact it's we boys who make the music, which is the cash-cow, we'd be surplus to requirements.

The meeting drags on with barely any input from me, Robbo, Bill, or Flaky. We trawl over estimated revenue, profit-and-loss sheets, fancy pie charts, and graphs. Julie shows us two cover designs for our next album.

'Jackie, can you send these designs out to our newsletter subscribers and ask them to vote on which one they prefer?' Julie asks.

'Yes, not a problem. It will have to be Sunday though, as I've set aside tomorrow to organise Geordie's fortieth birthday party. I need to get the invites out and the caterers are calling around.'

'That's fine,' Julie says. 'There's no rush since we don't have a release date for the album.'

'That's right. Will, can you give us some idea of when you think the album will be ready?'

Bill's glum face comes into shot. 'Not sure,' he mumbles. 'It's hard to say. We've got demos down for eight tracks. We'll need another four at least, maybe six if we want to include some bonus material. When Geordie comes down next week, I'll have a better idea.'

'Can you at least give me a guesstimate, a ballpark date?'

'I don't know... maybe November. We're dealing with the creation of songs not manufacturing widgets,' he grumbles.

Jackie tries to remain upbeat. 'November is a little late, Will. If we want to harvest the Christmas market, then we really need some finished product by the end of September at the latest to give us enough time to organise everything.'

I nearly fall off my chair, and quickly hit the mute button on the laptop.

'Christ, woman! I've told you before not to use the word—product—when talking to Bill about his music.'

Jackie winces and mimes the word, sorry, but it's too late. Billy has already launched a counter-offensive. For the next five minutes he goes off on a tirade about how music is not a product, or a commodity. It's not churned out in a factory like baked beans on a conveyor belt. He explains (for the umpteenth time) he doesn't write songs based upon profit-and-loss ledgers or calendar dates.

As he finally ends an embarrassed silence descends.

Jackie coughs and unmutes the laptop. 'Ahem, I'm sorry, Will. I didn't mean it like that. I was using the term—product, to encapsulate everything we sell, from CDs, digital downloads, vinyl, T-shirts, cups, posters, and keyrings, without having to list them individually.'

'Bloody keyrings,' he mumbles. 'What are we? A rock band or a fucking corporate accountancy firm?'

'Take no notice of him, Jackie,' Fiona starts. 'He's been like a bear with a sore head all day, a right bloody grump.'

'Okay,' Jackie replies, 'has anyone got anything else they'd like to discuss? John, any news about the Bloom tape and Heidelberg? I saw on the news the other day the creep got sentenced to twenty-five years.'

'Actually there is some good news on that front,' John replies. 'I have a meeting with one of his people next week. As discussed before, Heidelberg set up a new company and transferred all assets from the old one to the new one. He then dissolved the old company and resigned from the board of the new one prior to the rape trial.'

'He's despicable,' Flaky says angrily. 'He obviously did that to protect his assets from a civil lawsuit. Is it even legal?'

'It's definitely immoral, whether it's illegal—that's another matter. The upshot is, he's asset rich but cash poor. He's appealing the verdicts and that's going to cost him a lot of money. The fact a director of the new company contacted me and is flying out from LA to meet with me bodes well. I think he'll make an informal offer to sell the rights to the Bloom album back to us.'

'How much do you think they'll ask for?' Robbo queries.

'Probably the same amount they paid for it, which was six-hundred-thousand, US dollars,' John replies.

'We're not going to pay that much for it!' Bill snaps.

'Bill, that album is legendary, and only a handful of people have heard it. It will sell like hot cakes. The pre-orders alone would repay the outlay, and it's ready to go,' I offer.

'Yes,' John says, 'but Will is right, we won't be paying that for it. We are in the box seat. The album is useless to them without the accompanying film, which I'm sure will never be re-released. Like I said, Heidelberg is broke. He'll take whatever he can. There'll be the usual game of bluff and counter-bluff. But I've already seen their cards. I think a hundred grand would see the album safely back in your hands.'

'Wow!' Jackie and the other women coo.

'And in some other good news, next June will mark twenty years since you signed your first deal with GMC records, which means all rights to your songs will revert to you.'

'Christ!' I yell. 'We are about to make some serious money. We'll be able to put out our own greatest hits album next year.'

'There's no way I'm putting out a greatest hits album,' Bill barks. 'We're not some cheap novelty act?'

I share a knowing glance with Jackie.

'That's not your decision alone to make, is it?' Flaky says in a condescending tone. 'You are but one vote out of nine.'

'And lastly,' John continues, jumping in before the argument escalates, 'a more intriguing situation has arisen. I have an old friend called Jerry Bloomberg. I went to university with his son. Jerry is executive producer of the reality TV show—I Will Survive. I'm not sure if any of you have seen it?'

'Oh, aye. That's one of my favourite shows. Never miss it,' I reply excitedly.

'Me and Julie occasionally sit down to watch it,' Robbo says.

'Except we miss half of it because Robbo's in charge of the remote control. He spends most of the time flicking through all the channels,' Julie complains.

'It's the adverts. I can't stand them,' Robbo counters.

'I've seen it,' Flaky says. 'It sometimes feels a little contrived.'

'Good, good,' John continues. 'Well, I had an interesting conversation with Jerry a couple of days ago. They are doing preliminary work for the next season of the show. This time it's going to be a celebrity version. They're planning to have four teams of four, all pitted against each other. And he wanted to know...'

'If the Shooting Tsars would like to be in it?' Fiona says, ending John's sentence for him.

'Yes,' John says. 'It's early days, but he asked me to put the feelers out.'

'You can put your feelers away,' Bill grizzles.

'Hang on a minute,' I begin. 'I'd love to be on that show. It would be a great laugh.'

'A celebrity version, eh?' Flaky ponders. 'Do the winners get to donate the prize money to a charity of their choosing?'

'Yes, they do,' John says. 'One million pounds. A not inconsiderable sum.'

'I think it's a great idea,' Gillian pipes up. 'Think of what the Outreach Centre could do with one million pounds, Flaky.'

'I know. I'm having the same thoughts.'

'Absolutely no way! I will not, under any circumstances, be taking part in a celebrity jerk circle in some godforsaken hellhole. End of story,' Bill shouts.

'Wait up, Billy Boy. I think this warrants further discussion. Let's look at the pros, shall we? We could time the release of an album to coincide with the airing of the show. I Will Survive has some of the biggest ratings on TV. This is free publicity. Plus, it would be an experience of a lifetime. Don't dismiss it out of hand.'

'Geordie, you're speaking out of your arse cheeks. Robbo, what do you think?' Bill asks.

He's looking for an ally to repudiate the idea and Robbo's his best chance. He struggles to get out of bed in the morning. There's no way he'd relish a few weeks in dystopia.

Julie throws her hat into the ring before he answers. 'Robbo, I think it's a brilliant idea. You've been talking for years about getting off the booze, the fags, and the weed—well, here's your chance. It will be like detox,' she says.

'You know what, Jules, I think you might be right. It could be the kick-start I need.'

'Fuck me drunk,' Bill sighs wearily.

'Okay,' John begins, 'we may be getting a little ahead of ourselves. There'd be a lot of hoops to jump through before it was signed off on.'

'What sort of hoops?' Fiona asks.

'The chaps would all have to pass medicals and undergo a psychological assessment, and that's just the start.'

'Ha! There's no way Robbo would pass a medical. They'd be lucky to find a pulse,' Bill scoffs.

'Bullshit!' Robbo exclaims. 'I'm fitter than you are.'

'Yeah, dream on. You get out of puff lifting a cup of tea.'

'Will, you need to think of the greater good here,' Flaky intervenes. 'Think of a struggling charity receiving one million pounds. I think it's about time this band gave something back to society.'

'We do plenty of charity gigs. No, I'm warning you all, this is a bad idea. We can barely survive in five-star luxury hotels when we're on tour. How are we going to survive in some sweltering jungle or desert?'

'At least let's investigate further. We're not committing to anything at this stage,' I say.

'Okay, whatever,' Bill replies, thoroughly pissed off. There's a stilted silence for a moment. 'Right, is the meeting over?' he growls.

'One last thing,' Jackie says. 'My workload over the last eighteen months has almost doubled, and I'm struggling to find a work—life balance. From next week onwards, I'll be taking Tuesdays off. I think it's time we brought in some outside help. I suggest a virtual assistant. What do you all think?'

There is unanimous agreement amongst everyone, apart from Bill, who remains silent.

'Bill, your thoughts?' I ask.

'Yeah, I'm cool with that. I know all the girls get overwhelmed at times.'

'Good,' Jackie says. 'It's agreed, then. I'll start looking for someone. Right, meeting finished. Love you all, speak soon.'

There's another minute of repeated goodbyes before the screen goes blank. Jackie takes a big swig of lukewarm tea.

'Christ almighty! What the hell was stuck up Will's arse today?'

'He was a tad grumpy.'

'A tad grumpy! Miserable old twat!' she spits.

'I'm still online, you know... I can hear you.' Bill's voice echoes through the ether, followed by cackling laughter from Fiona.

Jackie clasps her hand over her mouth and turns bright red.

'I told you online meetings don't work,' I say with a cocky smile.

Chapter Six

Life's a Walk In The Park

I'm in the kitchen preparing breakfast as Jackie walks in. She has a cheeky grin on her face.

'What are you so happy about?' I ask slipping two slices of bread into the toaster.

'Have you forgotten? It's Tuesday!' she shouts, throwing her arms up in the air.

I smile. 'Oh, aye, I'd forgotten. It's your official day off.'

'Yes! An entire day to myself to do whatever I want.'

I pour her a black coffee as she takes a seat at the kitchen bench. 'How will you spend your first day of freedom?'

'I have my gym gear in my backpack and a book. I'm going to saunter down the high-street and grab a coffee and read for a while. Then I'll head to the gym. After that, I may do a spot of window shopping, and oh, I'm meeting Carly for lunch. I haven't caught up with her in weeks. Apparently, she's got herself a new man, so I'm looking forward to hearing all about him.'

I reflect carefully. 'Carly? Is she the one...'

'Yes, she's the one with the large breasts. Why do men always fixate on a woman's physical attributes to identify them?' she scolds.

'Excuse me, but I wasn't even going to mention her breasts—despite their size.'

'Really? What were you going to say then?' She eyes me suspiciously as she sips her coffee.

'I was going to say, is she the one who talks at a hundred miles an hour? The one that's dizzy?'

'Yes, that's Carly. She's not really dizzy, just excitable. After lunch, I may head to the market and get something for our dinner.'

'I'm pleased for you. You deserve it.'

She winces and appears contrite.

'What's the matter?' I ask.

'I feel guilty. It's not fair on you. You don't get a day off.'

I place my hands on her arms.

'I get plenty of time off. When I'm down at Bill's gaff recording or rehearsing. That's my free time.'

'But it's not though, is it? That's your work, your job.'

I laugh. 'It's not work. It's enjoyable and while I'm there, I don't do any chores apart from occasionally help with dinner. And it's not all sitting in a recording studio for twelve hours a day. We often go for a walk or to the pub when the creative juices are running low.' I kiss her on the forehead. 'No more guilt, right?'

She grins. 'Okay, no more guilt.'

'Promise?'

'I promise.'

'Good.'

'And what are your plans for the day?' she asks.

'I'll clean up the breakfast things, have a kickabout outside with the boys, then let them watch some TV. I may take them to the park about lunchtime. Let them burn some energy off. Hopefully, they'll have a sleep this afternoon.

⟫⟫⟫ ⟪⟪⟪

With the paper unfurled, I skip past the usual headlines of woe and destruction, violence, celebrity meltdowns and navigate to the racing guide. It's been a while since I had a flutter on the horses, and as I study the form, I get a slight tingle in my belly.

I'm sitting on a park bench in front of the kids' playground and occasionally raise my head to cast a watchful eye over my boys. Bobby is running around the perimeter of the play area with arms spread wide, pretending to be an aeroplane. Wallace is on the monkey bars, swinging from bar to bar. All is well.

After ten minutes studying the form guide, I pull out my mobile and hit my local bookies number.

'Caledonia Bookies,' announces a gruff, tobacco scarred voice.

'Is that you, Ted?'

'Aye.'

'It's me, Geordie.'

'Ah, Geordie! It's been a while. I wondered how long it would take you. When was your last bet... about eighteen months ago?'

I chuckle. 'And the rest,' I begin. 'I reckon it would be nigh on three years.'

'They all come back in the end,' Ted chortles.

'You make it sound like an addiction,' I scoff.

'It is my son. It is. Not that I'm one to condemn anyone for their fallibilities. So, what's your bet?'

'If I remember rightly, I still have about £400 in my account.'

'Hang on... I'll check.' There's a moment's pause, followed by a hacking cough. 'Yep, you have£424.57 in there.'

'Good. Stick £400 on—Take It Easy, running the 3:10 at Kempton. On the nose.'

'You realise it's a maiden, and the odds are twenty-to-one?'

'Aye, I'm well aware of that.'

'Okay, Geordie... your loss,' he laughs.

'I'll be in tomorrow morning to collect my winnings.'

'Dream on, big fella, but it's good to have you back,' he says as he hangs up.

I'm so engrossed in studying the form guide I barely notice someone come and sit on the far end of the bench. I eventually lift my head and consider the individual. It's a teenage boy. His clothes have seen better days. No trendy labels or designer gear, just drab, cheap apparel. His hands are stuffed into his trouser pockets and his thighs constantly twitch as his arched feet push his legs up and down in an agitated fashion. I fold my newspaper and place it on the bench.

'How yer going?' I ask.

He throws me a sideways glance. 'What the fuck has it got to do with you?' he responds sullenly, with no malice.

I'm puzzled by his response. 'There's no need to bloody swear.'

'Hypocrite,' he says. 'It's okay for you to swear but not me?'

'When you pass the age of sixteen, you can swear as much as you like... until then, watch your mouth.'

'I'll be sixteen soon enough.'

'Good for you.' He doesn't respond and returns his gaze to the ground. 'What's the problem?'

He stares at me again. 'Are you a paedo or what?'

'No, I'm not a paedo. Those two lads playing on the monkey bars are my sons.'

'That proves nothing,' he mumbles. 'Paedo's can have kids,' he retaliates as he throws a quick glance over his shoulder towards the playground.

'You're right, I suppose they can. But I was sitting here first. It was you who came and sat on my bench, not the other way around.'

'So you own the park benches now, do you?'

'You've got a serious attitude problem. What's made you so bitter and angry?'

'What do you care?'

'I don't care. I'm inquisitive.'

'You mean nosey.'

'Same thing. Are you in some sort of trouble?'

He lets out a deep sigh and slumps back in the bench but doesn't reply. I cast my eye across the park and spot two other lads heading our way. I pick up my paper.

As the two lads near, one of them calls out. 'Oi! Nobby no-mates!'

The boy next to me winces and emits a low groan as he slumps further into the park bench.

'Hey fuckwit, what are you doing here? You turned into a rent boy now?'

The three of them are of similar age and obviously know each other. One is tall and skinny; the other is short and stocky. They are both dressed in all the latest fashion gear. The boy on the bench ignores them and stares solemnly at the ground, averting his gaze.

'Scotty fuckwit, he's talking to you?' says the stocky lad as he kicks at the boy's feet.

'Fuck off and leave me alone,' he mumbles.

'Touchy, touchy. What's wrong with you? On your period?' mocks the taller lad.

I stand up and ponder my options carefully considering what has recently happened.

'Guess what boys? It's my fortieth birthday soon.'

My irrelevant statement stalls the situation as all three, eye me suspiciously.

'What do you want... a round of applause?' replies the skinny, tall lad.

'No. I'm simply making you aware I've been on this planet a lot longer than you, and I've learnt a few things. I'll freely admit I've still a long way to go, but here's the number-one lesson of life...'

The boys become interested, as though I'm going to teach them the fundamentals of alchemy. The seconds tick by.

'Go on then, what is it?' the stocky lad asks.

'If you cause shit to happen, then shit will happen to you.'

'What drugs are you on?' the skinny lad says, appearing confused and wary.

I smile at him. He takes a step back. 'All I'm saying is, life is bloody tough at the best of times, so why make it any tougher?'

My inarticulate, philosophical words of wisdom have unnerved the lads and they turn on their heels and head away.

'Fucking nutjob,' one of them hisses.

'Thanks,' the lad on the bench murmurs.

'No problem,' I say, dropping onto my seat. 'I take it you must be Scotty?'

The boy nods. 'Yep. Scotty Rafferty.'

'Good name.'

'Why?'

'You never heard of Gerry Rafferty?'

'No.' He shakes his head as he stares nervously down the street.

'Check him out. A great singer songwriter from Glasgow.'

'Okay. I will'

'Let me introduce myself; my name is...'

'I know who you are. You're Geordie, Geordie Kincaid from The Shooting Tsars.'

'Ah, you're a fan then?'

'Don't flatter yourself.'

'Okay... you're not a fan.'

'I didnae say that either,' he replies grumpily.

I'm losing patience with the boy. 'No, you didn't. But it's hard to know what you think because you don't say much.'

More silence ensues. I let out a deep sigh and shuffle, as though I've had enough.

'You going then?' he asks.

'Aye. The bairns have been here a while. They'll be getting hungry.'

He sits up straight and stares at me. 'What's it like being rich and famous?'

'It's amazing—ninety per cent of the time. No money worries. I live in the lap of luxury. I can buy whatever I want, although to be honest, I'm not one for toys and gadgets. I work when I want. I go to some fabulous places. People are queuing up with offers for autobiographies, guest spots on TV and radio for which I get paid more for an hour's work than most people would earn in a month. I get invited to celeb parties and offered the best seats at the best gigs and restaurants. It's wonderful. I'd be lying if I said any differently.'

He laughs. 'At least you're honest. I expected you to come out with bullshit about pressure and privacy. You said ninety per cent of the time—what's the bad ten per cent?'

'When I'm in the supermarket and the weans are playing up and someone comes and asks for a selfie.'

'You don't like selfies?'

'Loathe them with a passion.'

'So what do you do?'

'I give them a selfie. They're fans, or one of their family is a fan. They put me where I am to today. I always oblige. As painful as a selfie is, it's not like I'm working a twelve-hour shift in a coal mine.'

The lad becomes animated. 'How did you get to where you are? I mean, these days all you have to do is win some crummy TV talent show and you're a star, but I guess they didn't have that sort of thing back in your day.'

'You'd be surprised. Those sorts of shows have always been around in one format or another. But to answer your question; my life changed when I first met the other lads in the band. They were pretty ropey at first. I'm not sure they'd actually ever played a gig together. Anyway, once I'd heard Billy's songs at the audition...'

'Billy? You mean Will Harding?'

I nod. 'Aye. I knew he had something. His songs were rough diamonds, but diamonds, nonetheless. We rehearsed four hours a night, six nights a week for five months. That's not including the time I spent over at his ma's house, or he came over to my gaff to work on things.

Our first gig was played to three men and a Jack Russell in a working men's club in a rundown suburb of Leeds. They kept calling out if we knew any Frank Sinatra. Within six weeks, we were one of the best bands in Leeds. Two months later—*the* best band in Leeds. Another couple of months and we were the best band in the north of England. Then we got a manager, then a deal, and the rest is history.'

'Wow! That easy!'

'No! Not easy at all. I remember the nights when I'd finish my shift behind the bar and head home to my flat. Bill would be waiting on my front step, strumming away. He'd say he had a couple of great new songs and wanted to work on them while they were still fresh. We'd order in a couple of takeaway pizzas and grab a beer from the fridge. I can't tell you how many times I saw the sunrise as we sat rehearsing, refining, tinkering.

We lived in each other's pockets for months on end. It was during that time that we developed a deep friendship, but something else happened.'

'What?'

'A musical understanding. It was like a chemistry experiment that came together. Two completely different ingredients, that when mixed in the right amounts, became something new, bright, beautiful, majestic.

We spent the next three years either on the road or in the studio, not to mention the never-ending interviews, and photo and video shoots. I reckon we must have had about two weeks off in those first three years. It was unrelenting, energy-sapping, and mad as fuck. But I enjoyed every minute.'

'You sound like you miss it... those early days?'

I reflect. 'Yes and no. It was a baptism of fire. It either makes or breaks you. When you're eighteen years old, you have a lot fewer responsibilities, a lot more energy, and you don't give a damn about anything. I miss the freedom. I miss my youth, but I wouldn't change it for what I've got now.

Anyway, enough about me... what's happening in your life?'

Scotty rubs his hands together as troubled thoughts crease his brow. 'My life is shit. Has been since the day I was born, and I can't ever see it changing.'

'Are you sure you're not just having a bad day and feeling sorry for yourself?'

'Quite sure.'

'What is it? School, are you being bullied, girlfriend trouble?'

He scuffs at the pavement with the sole of his shoe. 'No.'

'Parents?'

He puffs out air. 'Not my ma... she's an angel.'

'I see. It's your old man, then?'

'Yeah, he's a bastard. A drunken bum. An alcoholic, abuser.'

Christ, I'm getting in deep now, maybe a little too deep. 'Abuser? In what way?'

'Verbal, physical, mental... you name it, he's a master of it.'

'Sexual?'

'Nah, none of that stuff.'

More silence.

'Does he knock you around?'

'Aye, at least he used to. But I don't care for myself. It's my ma that breaks me up.'

'You said, used to. Not anymore?'

'He's taken his belt to me since I can remember. The buckle end.'

He turns his palms upward to show me his inner forearms. They are laced with white scars and welts that have healed over. 'I have them all over; on my back, my legs, my arse.'

'Jeez,' I whisper.

'He tried it again about six weeks back. Came home hammered from the pub. Started ranting and raving, throwing things about, then started rummaging through my bedroom for things to sell.'

'What sort of things?'

'Anything he can flog down the pub or take to the second-hand shops. That's where my guitar went. It was a birthday present from my mam for my twelfth birthday. I cherished it. It wasn't anything flash, just a cheap acoustic copy, but I loved it. It was my escape mechanism.

One day I came home, and it was gone. Anyway, that night he's on the rampage again and I told him to get out of my bedroom and never come in again. His eyes stood out on stalks. It's the first time I'd ever stood up to him. He slammed my bedroom door shut and whipped off his belt. Said he was going to give me the thrashing of my life.

Something snapped in me. I knew I had to make a stand, or this would go on forever, or at least until I left, which I would have done a long time ago if it wasn't for my mother. He hit me once, but I caught the end of the belt. I pulled him towards me and punched him right on the end of the nose. He went down like a sack of shit, blabbing like a bairn, clutching his nose. Big tough man didn't like the taste of his own medicine. I told him if he ever lifted another finger to me or my ma, I'd kill him, and I didn't care about the consequences. It's the worst. Sometimes I wish it were over. If it weren't for me ma, it would be. I can't leave her behind, not with that bastard.'

I suffer an unwelcome flashback to my early childhood and am overcome with a sense of grief and horror. He sniffs and quickly wipes at the wetness on his cheek, embarrassed.

Sweet merciful Lord! A wee lad already wishing his life away. Come on, Geordie, dig deep... think!

'You can't talk like that. If you kill yourself or him, he wins.'

He lifts his head and stares at me. 'What do you mean?'

'You end up with a fifteen to twenty year prison sentence. And prison is no place for a young lad. By the time you come out, your youth will be over. You'll be on a road to damnation. No job, no trade, no money. Like I say, he wins.'

He gazes at the ground. 'Life shouldn't be like this, should it? I know people have their ups and downs, but no one should be miserable all the time, especially because of someone else.'

I try to change the subject. 'So you play the guitar?'

'Used to.'

'Any good?'

He shrugs. 'I guess. I've written a few songs. Never played them to anyone though, apart from me ma.'

'I always liked the school holidays; a chance to earn some cash. Do you have a part-time job? '

'I did have but gave it away.'

'Why?'

'No point. *He* always stole my money. I'd give some to mam, and he'd steal it from her purse. I'd hide it in my bedroom, and he'd always find it. Anyway, I've wasted enough of your time. Pleased to meet you, and by the way—I am actually a big fan of the Tsars. I'd like to say I had all your albums on CD, but you know who sold them as well, so I can only listen to you on music streaming.'

He lifts himself from the bench and shakes my hand, then saunters off.

'Wait!' I cry. 'Come back. I want a word.'

He reluctantly shuffles back.

'What?'

I prod him gently in the chest. 'Music—you said it was your escape mechanism?'

'Aye.'

'Good. Now make it your escape route.'

'I don't follow?'

'You have something about you. A flame that has not yet been extinguished. Nurture it above all else. However bad things seem now, they will change if you make them change. And believe me, things can change quickly. Just keep believing.'

'In what?'

'In yourself, to make the right choices.'

He ponders the words before half-turning to leave again. 'Cheers, Geordie.'

'Hey, how are you for money?'

'I don't want charity.'

'I'm not offering you charity. I'm offering you a shitty job, with surprisingly good money. Interested?'

'Told you; no point.'

'I thought you were smart, but maybe you're not,' I add with a frown.

'What's that supposed to mean?'

I tap at my head. 'Upstairs for thinking, downstairs for dancing. Open a bank account, get a debit card, and keep it on you all the time. That way, he cannae take your money, can he?'

He tilts his head to one side. 'Suppose not. What's this shitty job?'

'I need my lawn mowing once a week at the moment, plus an hour or two weeding. And there are plenty of other jobs I need doing; painting, pressure washing... just odd jobs.'

'How much you paying?'

'How does twenty-five quid an hour sound?'

A grin lights up his face. 'You gotta be joking?'

'I kid you not.'

'Okay, you're on. When do you want me to start?'

I laugh as I pick up my paper, scribble down my address and mobile number on the bottom of the page, then rip it off and hand it to him.

'Come around tomorrow afternoon, about three, and we'll sort things out.'

He stares at the address. 'Shit! You must be seriously loaded living there. Okay, tomorrow at three.'

We shake hands once more.

'Cheers, Geordie. I won't let you down,' he says with a beam on his face.

'I don't care if you let me down. Just don't let yourself down. Go on now, skedaddle.'

He turns and jogs across the playground and into the park with a bounce in his step. I watch in silence as his figure disappears from view.

'The world is a crazy fucked up place,' I murmur.

I return my attention to the form guide—but not for long.

'Geordie! How are you this fine day?' The voice is recognisable as I wearily lift my head up. It's Constable Dankworth and Constable Constable on their beat.

'It would be a lot better if I wasn't constantly interrupted. Can a man get no peace and tranquillity these days?'

'Was that lad bothering you?' Dankworth asks.

'No. Why do you ask?'

'He's a bad 'un,' Constable says.

'The apple doesn't fall far from the tree,' Dankworth agrees.

'Is that so?' I reply.

'Stealing cars, breaking and entering. Not that we've ever caught him in the act,' Constable explains.

'But we know it's him,' Dankworth adds, as he rocks gently back and forth on his heels.

'Based on what evidence?' I ask.

'We have our sources,' Dankworth replies, giving me a sneaky wink.

'We have contacts in the underworld,' Constable continues in an overly officious voice. He taps the end of his nose. 'Can't say too much. Loose words cost lives.'

'The lad seems okay to me. He seems down about things, but he didn't come across as Baby Face Nelson.'

'Appearances can be deceptive, Geordie. When you've been on the force as long as Constable Dankworth and I have you develop a second sense. Mind you, I can't really blame the lad. We're always around at his place on domestic violence reports. The old man's a drunken, worthless bum. Likes to knock his missus around. She always takes him back though, God knows why.'

'Hmm... I see. I've actually given the lad a job mowing my lawn.'

Dankworth and Constable grimace.

'I'm not sure that's a good idea, Geordie. He'll case your joint,' Constable says.

'The lad deserves a break.'

The two coppers snigger. 'You don't know human nature very well,' Dankworth begins. 'When you've dealt with scum as long as Constable Constable and I have, you learn not to trust anyone. Try to lend a helping hand and they'll steal your wristwatch.'

'Really... well, don't let me keep you,' I state.

'Okay, well don't say we didn't warn you.'

As they depart I glance over at Wallace and Robert, who still seem happy to be at the playground, but my stomach is rumbling.

'Hey, boys! Another five minutes, then we're leaving. We need to get some lunch.'

A chorus of disapproval flies my way.

'Yoo-hoo! Geordie!' a female voice cries out.

I turn around and spot an attractive woman heading my way. I don't instantly recognise her until she's standing in front of me, then my memory kicks in. She has two assets that aren't easy to forget.

'Hi Carly, how are you doing?'

'I'm doing fine. How about you? You look good. Oh, there are the boys on the swings. Wallace, Robert, yoo-hoo!' she shouts and waves madly at them.

They both offer an uncertain wave back.

'Oh, they grow so quickly, don't they?'

'Yes, they...'

'It's been a while since I saw you. What have you been up to? Keeping busy?'

'Yes, I've...'

'Have you any new music coming out? Last time I saw you, you were working on a new album?'

'Yes, we've...'

'Oh, sorry to interrupt, but I've some splendid news of my own. I've got myself a new fella. He's the manager at the Safeway supermarket, you know the big one in the centre?'

'I...'

'We met in the meat aisle next to the Cumberland sausages. It was love at first sight. We've been going steady now for over a month. I'm walking on air.' She stops to draw breath and glances at her watch. 'Oh, damn it! It's nearly one. I'm running late. I'd love to stop and chat, but I need to get back to the office. Tell Jackie I'll call her at the weekend. We really must have a catch up. I haven't seen her in ages. I miss her.'

'But you were...'

'Must dash. See ya, boys!'

The lads ignore her this time.

'It's been lovely to chat, Geordie.'

She pecks me on the cheek and walks off at a brisk pace. I'm bemused by the incident.

'This has been a relaxing hour in the park. I really should do it more often,' I mutter.

Chapter Seven

The Lie

I'm busy in the kitchen prepping food as the front door slams shut.

'It's only me!' Jackie calls out.

A moment later, she bustles through the door laden down with bags of shopping. She kisses me on the cheek and dumps the bags on the table and kicks her shoes off.

'Oh, what a day I've had. It's been great. Freedom!' she cries, throwing her arms above her head. 'I feel like a new woman. I really do. It's like I've had my batteries recharged. Who would have thought something so simple could have such a positive effect? What are you up to? Where are my boys?'

'They're in the bath. I'm preparing their dinner now.'

'I've got some salmon steaks for us. Do you mind throwing a green salad together to go with it?'

'No, not at all. Give me a rundown of your day.'

She unpacks the bags and puts the groceries away into various cupboards.

'I got a coffee and read my book. Then did a spot of window shopping, then went to the gym.'

'Did you catch up with Carly?'

'Yes. We had lunch at that new Korean restaurant near the park.'

'Really?'

'Yes, it was pretty good.'

'What's it like? Is it like Chinese food?'

'A bit. But they have things like dried seafood and lots of pickles and spices. Everything's quite salty. You'd love it.'

'And how was Carly?'

'Oh, you know Carly, talking at ten to the dozen. Excited about her new boyfriend.'

'Where does he work?'

'Oh, erm, she didn't say, and I never asked.'

'What time did you have lunch?'

She pulls a puzzled expression. 'You're never usually this interested in what I've been doing.'

'I'm asking to see how long it is since you've eaten, then I know when to prepare dinner.'

'Oh, sorry. It was just after twelve and we were probably in there for the best part of an hour.'

'I see. Do you want dinner right now or later?'

'In about an hour, would be great if that suits you?'

'Sure.'

'Right, I'm going to pop upstairs and see the boys, then get a quick shower.'

She disappears from the room and races up the stairs with a spring in her step as a glut of emotions washes over me—confusion, jealousy, anger, and fear all jockey for position.

Why didn't I pull her up right there and then? Either Carly has dementia, or my wife just lied to me. Why would she lie? Why does anyone lie? To cover something up!

Chapter Eight

A Friend in Need

I'm in the back room of the bookies as Ted huffs and puffs as he counts out the money.

'I had to do a lot of running around getting this amount of cash together,' he grumbles. 'Right, eight grand. If you could count it, then sign this form to say you've collected your winnings, we'll be all done.'

I take the wad of one hundred pound notes from him and quickly tally them up, trying hard to hide my delight.

'Aye, all there. Eight big ones.'

I scribble my signature on the document, stick the notes back inside the manilla envelope, and slide it into my jacket pocket.

'Lucky bastard,' he moans.

'Come on Ted, you should be pleased I've returned to the fold. I'm sure you'll get all this back in time.'

He removes a stub of a rollie from his lips and coughs.

'Geordie, if I ever see your face again, it will be too soon.'

I chuckle and pat him on his wizened arm.

'Hey, it's only business... nothing personal.'

'Go on, get out, you big lummox. I'll let you out the back door,' he says with a half-smile.

I stroll down the alley and turn into the main high-street, feeling like a million dollars, or eight thousand pounds. There's a unique sensation about being paid out in cash from a bookmaker. It's comparable to Christmas morning when you're a kid. The thrill and excitement are magical. It's not like I need the money. In fact, it's irrelevant. It's simply down to the winning sensation of beating the system. The problem I have now is what to do with it. If I pay it into the bank, Jackie will spot it straight away. She's a financial hawk and studies the statements online at least twice a week to monitor things. My only option is to find a good hidey-hole at home, but if she finds it, there'll be hell to pay. I've got to think of a spot where she'll never look. I decide to head to the local coffee shop and get a brew and consider my possible hideaways.

As I turn into the doorway, a woman comes barging out and clatters into me. She ricochets off my chest and stumbles ungainly. I reach out and grab her before she hits the ground.

'Hey, you want to be more careful,' I advise.

She's in tears as she drags her forearm across her face. I'm concerned she may have injured herself.

'Are you alright?'

'Yes, I'm fine. I'm sorry,' she says, looking up at up at me. 'Oh, Geordie, it's you.'

'Sandra! Are you hurt?'

I'm as surprised as she is.

'No, no, I'm okay.'

'Then why are you crying?'

'Oh, it's nothing.'

'It must be something. Come on, I'll buy you a coffee and we can talk about it.'

I place the cups on the table and take a seat as Sandra noisily blows her nose. It's the first time I've seen her since Wallace's birthday, when I insulted her. Even though I apologised by phone, I still feel embarrassed at my outburst.

'You know, Sandra, I really am sorry about what I said to you at the party. It was out of character. The red mist had descended, and I lashed out at anyone who got in my line of vision. I didnae mean a word of it.'

'That's okay, Geordie. You were stressed. We can all say hurtful things we don't mean occasionally. It's not a big deal... really.'

She takes a sip of her coffee and sniffs.

'That's very magnanimous of you, Sandra. Right, so what's with all the tears?'

'You don't want to hear about my problems.'

'I wouldnae be sitting here if I didn't,' I reply as I place my hand on her arm and offer her a warm smile. 'Now come on, tell your Uncle Geordie what the matter is.'

'It's my landlord. He's given us until the end of the week to get out of the flat. I'm three months behind with the rent and it's not the first time it's happened. I don't blame him. He's not a charity. He's been incredibly good and understanding, but everyone has their limits.'

'Ah, I see. You're doing it tough?'

'Yes. It's difficult being a single mum. I can only do part-time work because of Ollie, and you know what kids are like. They're always getting sick at this age, which means I then have to miss my shift. And as for the school holidays, it's a nightmare! I spend more on childcare fees than I make from working. I've had ten different part-time jobs over the last two years.'

'What about the boy's father? Does he not help out?'

'Ha! I have had no contact with him since he left me four years ago. Last I heard, he was somewhere in the States with his bit of fluff. Anyway, I don't need him. It's just me and Ollie now.'

'What about social security?'

She blows her nose again on a tissue and takes a deep breath as she calms slightly.

'That's another nightmare. They make you jump through hoops. It's demeaning. I get a little help with housing benefit, but the more I earn, the less I receive. It's a catch twenty-two.'

'How much are you behind with your rent?'

'Three grand. I've no hope of ever catching up. I'm at my wit's end.'

I take a slurp of coffee. 'I tell you what, Sandra, I'll help you out. I've had a small win on the gee-gees.'

'How much?'

'Eight grand.'

She nearly spits her coffee out. 'Eight thousand pounds?'

'Aye. It's all yours.'

'Don't be silly. I couldn't possibly accept.'

'Why not?'

'Because...'

'Yes?'

'It's not right. You don't owe me. I'm not your problem.'

'You're sitting twelve-inches away from me, in a right lather; of course you're my problem,' I say with a chuckle. 'I mean it. I want you to take the money. You can settle your arrears and maybe pay a couple of months up front to give yourself some breathing space. A bit of time to reassess.' I tap the inside of my pocket. 'I have it on me now. We'll finish our coffee, then pay a visit to your bank and deposit it.'

Her face is deadpan, as if she's in shock. 'I don't know what to say. I'll pay you back... when I can. It might take a while.'

'Don't talk daft, woman! I'm not out of pocket. It's all the gamblers who lost their shirts yesterday who have kindly donated to your cause.'

She cracks a huge beam.

'That's better. You're far more attractive when you smile.'

'Geordie...'

'Not another word,' I say as I drain the dregs from my cup.

As we make our way along the busy high-street, I have a thought.

'Sandra, you should get together with Jackie and the other girls from the band,' I suggest.

'Why?'

'Because they're all canny businesswomen. Jackie's a master of designing websites and maintaining them. Julie's a brilliant graphic artist. Gillian is a wizard with accounting and money matters, and Fiona is a social media and email marketing expert.'

'I don't follow?'

'Well, I was thinking. You're into all that hippy and new-age malarky. You could open a shop. Create your own business selling trinkets, and homemade soap and all that other nonsense which you see at Sunday markets.'

She giggles. 'You're not a believer, are you?'

'Sorry. I didn't mean to be disparaging.'

'It's a good idea, Geordie, and there's definitely a market for that sort of stuff, but I'd imagine opening a shop would be very expensive and I'd still have the problem of juggling childcare, Ollie, and school holidays.'

I stop, grab her arm, and spin her around. 'I'm talking about an online store. You'd work the hours that suited you from home. Think about it; you'd be your own boss and you could sell to the world, not just local. You'd obviously need to have a good looking website with automatic payment and delivery options, and source suppliers, but the girls could help you out with all that. I'm not saying you'd make a fortune, but it may be enough to cover your living costs. Anyway, it was a thought. Chew it over and get together with Jackie to discuss it.'

Her gaze is distant. 'You could be onto something. I think it could work, but I'd need to do a lot of research.'

'That's the spirit. Oh, about the money?'

'You've changed your mind?' she says, wincing.

'No, of course not. But I'd appreciate it if you didn't mention to Jackie about my little windfall. I don't like keeping secrets from my wife, but she doesn't approve of gambling and if she found out, it would only cause an unnecessary argument.'

'Okay. Mum's the word,' she replies with a chuckle.

'Good. You've actually saved me from a bit of a dilemma.'

'How's that?'

'I was struggling to think of a suitable place to hide it.'

She gives me a peck on the cheek. 'Twenty minutes ago, I was a frightened woman, cowed by life. Now, I believe in the possibilities that are open to me. Thanks Geordie. I won't forget this.'

'They say that money isn't everything... and it's true. But it certainly helps. Right, come on. Let's get to the bank.'

Chapter Nine

Shrink Wrap

It's not a great start to the day.

'Geordie, you said you were going to seek help. It's been over a week, and you've done nothing about it,' Jackie says as she drops two teabags into cups and pours water from the kettle into them.

There's no malice or disappointment in her words, but there is a sense of urgency.

'Ahem, yes, I'll get on to it as soon as possible. I've been quite busy working on some song structures for a couple of new songs that Billy has demoed.'

She places the cups on the table, sits opposite and fixes me with a disbelieving stare.

The truth is, I've been procrastinating. I'm not one for navel gazing or trawling over past deeds to find my inner demons. Each day is a new day, a brand new start. There's too much of this self-help, let's find ourselves nonsense these days. My old Nan didn't believe in it. She had a catalogue of idioms and cliches to turn to when times were tough; "Don't worry, at the end of the day it will sort itself out;" "Better the devil you know;" "Tomorrow is another day;" and her favourite, "What goes around comes around," saved for people who would eventually get their comeuppance.

I could write a book based upon her old-school words of wisdom. I would title it, "My Nan Didn't Half Speak Some Crap!"

I'm not really sure why I'm stalling. Maybe I'm afraid of the unknown. Whatever the reason, Jackie is on to it.

'I know you're not keen on this sort of thing, and who knows, it might not be for you. But all I ask is that you give it a go. The boys are at a very impressionable age, and I don't want them growing up thinking sudden outbursts of aggression are acceptable. With that in mind, I've been doing some research.'

Her hand darts into her pocket and she pulls out a slip of paper and pushes it across the table.

'Dr John Galway. A trained psychologist with an excellent background. I've booked you in for a preliminary session this morning at ten. I've spoken with him on the phone, and he sounds like a delightful man. It's only one hour, so you can become acquainted, to see if you're both a good fit for each other.'

A good fit? What the hell does that mean? We're not a pair of bloody shoes.

'I'm a little busy today...' I begin, before she cuts me off.

'No, you're not. I've checked your diary. You have absolutely nothing on. You're going. That's the end of the matter. Remember what they say; a thousand-mile journey begins with one step. From little things big things grow.'

And there I have the sequel to my Nan's book—'All Knowing, All Seeing—My Wife and Other Omnipotent Angels.'

Dr Galway's practice is an old cottage overlooking the Firth of Forth. There's a cool breeze as I walk down the garden path and ring the bell. A few seconds later I'm confronted with the good doctor, himself.

'Aha! And you must be Geordie!' he declares, far too enthusiastically for my liking.

'Aye, correct,' I reply, as I run my eye over him.

He's dressed in flared khaki dungarees, and he's barefoot. His bushy, ginger beard matches his long wavy hair. I'd say he'd be in his early fifties.

'Please enter,' he says, flinging the door wide open.

I'm immediately hit by the heady aroma of aromatic oils.

'Please leave your shoes at the door.'

I kick my shoes off and enter and follow him down a hallway and into a room.

'Take a seat. I had an interesting conversation with your wife the other day. She sounds like a wonderful woman. She told me a lot about you.'

I gaze around the room looking for a chair but can't see one. There are, however, two giant pink beanbags positioned opposite each other in the centre of the room.

'My wife is particularly good at pointing out my shortcomings,' I chunter. 'She's not as good at seeing her own.'

He laughs. 'Do I detect a smidgen of resentment?'

I collapse into a beanbag. The aroma of patchouli oil is overwhelming. I hate the smell. If I'd ever had the misfortune to stick my nose into a tramp's underpants, then I imagine the scent would not be dissimilar.

'Not really,' I reply. 'Women think—men do.'

He flops down opposite me. 'Do you know women outlive men by over ten years? What do you think the reason for that is?'

'Because most women don't have wives,' I reply as I glance at the walls, which resemble a child's nursery with smiling clowns and various animals stencilled on the surface.

He chuckles again. 'No, nice theory though. Women express their emotions, whereas men repress them. Repressed emotion is a canker.'

'Really,' I mumble.

I've already decided this is a bad idea. I can't take anyone seriously who wears khaki dungarees, not unless they're a plumber.

'What's with the bean bags?' I ask.

'It brings us closer to Mother Earth. We can feel the vibrations as she breathes.'

He reaches to his right and picks up a set of small bells and gives them a shake.

'I think we'll start off with a purification ritual. Repeat what I do,' he instructs.

He crosses his legs and closes his eyes as the tips of his index fingers rest on his knees.

'Ommmmmmmm.... ommmmmmm....'

'Om,' I repeat, just the once.

One eyelid flicks open as he squints at me.

'Hmm... I see. Maybe we'll come back to that,' he says.

And maybe we won't.

'We'll try some laughter therapy. You'll enjoy this.'

I wouldn't bet your house on it, pal.

'I'll start off with a slight chuckle, followed by laughter, then heaving guffaws. Eventually, you'll follow suit. Within a few minutes, we'll both be rolling around on our sides with tears streaming down our faces. It releases the tension and sweeps away the barriers between us. It never fails.'

He closes his eyes, chortles. Within a few seconds, he's laughing like a drain. Slowly, it's replaced by rib-cracking guffaws. I stare at him, emotionless, not in the least bit amused. I've laughed harder at a funeral.

I push myself up from the beanbag, exit the room, walk down the hallway, and slip back into my shoes. I can still hear the halfwit inside, howling like a hyena.

⟫⟫ ⟪⟪

Jackie's annoyed with me.

'For God's sake, Geordie! You didn't even give him a chance!'

'He's a mad old hippy. Laughter therapy, vibrations from Mother Earth, and the overwhelming funk of patchouli oil is not my scene. We'll find someone else. There's no rush.'

She pulls a notepad from the kitchen drawer and flips it open. There's a list of about ten names neatly written in a column accompanied by telephone numbers. She takes her pen and strikes a line through one name.

'Okay, that's Dr Galway off the list. I will not let you prevaricate over this. I know you. If you don't like something, you run away from it.'

She picks up her mobile and dials. 'Oh, hello, my name is Jackie Kincaid, and I'm ringing on behalf of my husband. I'm hoping to set up an initial consultative appointment for him.'

The garden beckons. I wander outside and sit on the top step of the patio, unable to listen to my wife as she describes my failings with a complete stranger.

⤜⤛ ⤜⤛

I stare at the slip of paper Jackie handed me. Reluctantly, I leave the safety of my car and make my way up the steps of a modern town house and ring the bell. A plaque on the wall reads—Forbes Wellness Clinic. The door is flung open, and I'm confronted with a young, handsome man. Actually, he's more like a boy.

'Hi, I'm Geordie Kincaid, I have an appointment with Justin Forbes... life coach?'

He smiles and ushers me in. 'Come in, Geordie. We've been expecting you.' He grins as he closes the door.

Of course they've been expecting me, that's what happens when you make an appointment.

He shows me to a snug, tastefully decorated room. I flop down into a well-worn Chesterfield couch.

'Make yourself comfortable. Would you like a tea or coffee?' he asks.

'Aye, a black coffee, no sugar, would be nice, thanks.'

He nods and smiles at me, flashing a perfect set of pearly whites as he slips out of the room. I assume he's the receptionist or trainee.

How do you become a trainee in life coaching?

I tap on the arm of the couch feeling decidedly uncomfortable and apprehensive. A few minutes pass before he returns.

'Here we go. I've put a drop of cold in it for you.'

He hands me a cup and saucer and takes up position behind a desk opposite me. I throw a glance at the door, then return my gaze to him, puzzled.

'Erm... I think there's been a mistake.'

He smiles at me again. I'm already sick of his good cheer.

'Why's that?'

'I'm here to see Justin Forbes, life coach. Are you his son?' I ask taking a sip of coffee.

He laughs. 'No, I'm not his son. I'm Justin Forbes, your life coach.'

I cough and spit the coffee back out into the cup.

'Are you okay?'

'Ahem, yes. It's a little hot, that's all.'

'My apologies. Let's begin. How about you tell me why you're here and what you expect to get from your sessions?' he declares, leaning back in his chair as he twists a pencil around and around.

I place the cup and saucer on a side table and gaze at him. 'Before we start, I have a few questions.'

Again, with the smile. 'Fire away.'

'How old are you?'

'I'm twenty-three. Does my age bother you?'

Sweet merry Jesus!

'No, no, not at all, of course not...' I pause. 'Well, actually, yes... it bothers me.'

'Why?'

'Because you're twenty-three. How can you be a life coach? You've barely lived.'

'Jesus was only thirty when he began preaching and yet he changed the world forever,' he states, followed by his ghastly smile.

Okay, time to leave.

⤜⤜⤜ ⤛⤛⤛

Jackie's even more annoyed with me.

'He was barely out of nappies,' I explain. 'What can he possibly know about life at his age? When he compared himself to Jesus... well, that was it.'

She purses her lips as she glares at me. 'What did he say?'

'He said Jesus didn't start preaching until he was thirty.'

'That doesn't mean he was comparing himself to Jesus! He was merely highlighting age has nothing to do with experience or knowledge!'

'Age *is* experience and knowledge. They're one and the same. Anyway, you weren't there. I picked up a vibe.'

'What sort of vibe?' she asks as she furiously starts wiping down the kitchen countertop, a habit she turns to when fuming.

'You know... a born-again Christian type of vibe.'

'Don't talk daft!'

'I'm telling you. A few sessions with Tintin, and I'd have been praising the Lord and baptising Wallace and Robert in the waters of Leith.'

'Who the hell is Tintin?' she says, screwing her face up.

'You don't know who Tintin is? You'll be telling me next you've never heard of Popeye.'

'I haven't.'

I shake my head in disbelief as she pulls out her notepad and strikes through another name.

'Geordie, what are you looking for in a psychologist?'

I ponder her question for a moment as she stares at the list of practitioners.

'First of all, they have to be older than me.'

'How much older?'

'At least twenty years. Preferably, thirty or more.'

'Okay. So they have to be aged between sixty and one hundred and fifty.'

'Don't get shitty. And they have to be male. I'm not being sexist, but I'd feel more comfortable speaking with an older guy, that's all.'

'Anything else?' she asks as she strikes through names on her list.

'No hippies or new-age wankers. Oh, and it would help if they had a beard.'

She freezes. 'A beard. What has facial hair got to do with medical expertise?'

I shuffle uncomfortably. 'Nothing. It's just that... well... I don't know. It adds a certain gravitas.'

'Any preference for bushy eyebrows or beige cardigans? Maybe tartan slippers and a hot-water bottle, a wheelchair, and a crocheted blanket.'

'You're being ridiculous.'

'Ah, and I thought it was you who was being ridiculous.' She re-focuses her attention onto the notepad. 'Right, that leaves one name. Dr Engle has a practice in Bilston Glen. An expert in a technique called primal therapy. He has an excellent reputation, but he's semi-retired so it may be difficult to get in with him.'

'Dr Engle?' I murmur as an unwelcome thought flits across my mind. 'Wasn't he something to do with the Nazis and the death camps?'

'Don't even dare!' she snaps as she picks up her mobile phone.

❧ ❧

I saunter into the kitchen and drop the car keys on the countertop. Jackie is busily cleaning the oven while Wallace and Robert watch TV. I walk up behind Jackie and kiss her on the neck.

'I see you have the yellow rubber gloves on. Are you deliberately trying to tease me?' I whisper into her ear.

She elbows me away. 'If you think rubber gloves are sexy, there's something wrong with you. Did you forget to tell me something?'

I fill a glass with water and knock it back.

'It's warm out there,' I say as I wipe the drips on the back of my hand. 'Did you hear me?'

'What? No, I haven't forgotten to tell you anything.'

'Look outside... in the garden.'

I stare out of the window and spot Scotty filling the lawn mower with petrol.

'Oh, yes! I forgot. The lad's called Scotty. I'm employing him for the summer to cut the grass and do a spot of weeding. When did he arrive?'

'About thirty minutes ago. How do you know him?'

'I met him on a park bench.'

She stops scrubbing the oven and turns to me. 'You mean he's a complete stranger?'

'Not anymore.'

She pulls a severe frown. 'We have two young boys in the house.'

'So?'

'I'm not happy with an unknown adolescent frequenting our home. He could be into drugs.'

'You don't mind Robbo visiting.'

'He's not an adolescent.'

'No, his intellect has not reached that stage yet. Anyway, the lad's not into drugs. He's doing it tough. An abusive father, no mates, and no money. I thought he needed a break.'

She eyes me warily before returning her attention to the oven. I grab a chilled can of ginger beer from the fridge and a packet of crisps from the pantry and head outside. He doesn't notice me, so I stand and watch him for a while. He's doing a decent job under warm conditions. The boy is as skinny as a rake. He should be filling out a little at his age, but he appears malnourished. Sunken cheeks sit below grey bags under his eyes. As he gets to the end of the garden and spins around, I hold up the refreshments and waggle them to catch his attention. He turns off the mower and ambles over to me, smiling shyly.

'Geordie, how yer going?'

'I'm good, mate. Here, take these and have a breather,' I say as I pass him the drink and crisps.

'Cheers.'

He sits on the top step of the patio, cracks open the can and takes three lusty slurps before starting on the crisps.

'You seem a little better in yourself today,' I say.

'I guess. It's because I have something to do.'

'We all need a purpose in life.'

Chapter Ten

Time Out

I knock on the door and let myself in. 'Hey, Billy Boy, where are you?'

'I'm out the back, on the deck!' comes his reply. I place my bag down in the hallway, make my way to the back door, and let myself out into the garden. Caesar usually comes bounding up to me, but he's noticeable by his absence. Bill is sitting on a chair next to a garden table, gently strumming his acoustic guitar.

'Where's Caesar?' I ask as I pull up a seat. He props his guitar against the table and pulls out his smokes.

'He's with Fiona and the kids. They're in Pugstow visiting her mum and my mum. They're due back at the weekend, so that gives us three good days to crack on with things. Have you eaten?'

'Yeah, got some takeaway junk on the way down.'

'Okay, let's get straight into it. The studio's all set up.' He stands up and lights a smoke.

'Erm, the thing is. I'm not really in the mood at the moment,' I reply sheepishly.

'That's not like you. Okay, well what do you want to do?' he says, puffing smoke out into the warm summer's air.

I point at the Inglegor Pike in the distance.

'What about a walk up that hill of yours?'

He does a double take and eyes me warily. 'Fuck me! What's got into you?'

'I don't know... it may help me unwind a bit.'

His brow furrows. 'Is everything okay? I thought Jackie had forgiven you about your outburst at the birthday party?'

'Yeah, she has.'

'Is anything else the matter?'

'No, of course not. Can't a man want a relaxing walk without being interrogated?' I snap.

'Okay, fine. I'll make some sandwiches and a flask of tea. Say, half an hour and we'll head off?' I nod my approval. 'You take your bag up to the guest bedroom and I'll crack on. I hope you've got some proper walking boots?'

He's already disappeared back inside. I stare into the distance and try to push the yawning sadness back down into the pit of my stomach.

⤜⤛

As we pass the Beaconsfield Arms, we resist the temptation to call in for a quick pint. It isn't long before we are on the foothills of Inglegor Pike. The vast open space and greenery releases something in me. For the first time since Jackie's lie, a pang of optimism momentarily lifts my spirits. I don't know why, because in reality, my setting hasn't changed a single thing. Nevertheless, it's pleasant to feel an emotion that isn't anger or sadness.

As we stride briskly up the hill, we talk about music, our kids, my forthcoming birthday, all the usual things. Nothing heavy, just light, and breezy chit-chat between two good pals.

'Flaky and Gillian called in last week for a couple of hours,' I remark.

'Oh, how come?' Bill replies.

'They were visiting one of Flaky's cousins who lives in Aberdeen. As they were passing, they popped in for a cuppa.'

'How are they?'

'Yeah, good. Flaky's tolerable when it's one on one. He's like a different person.'

'Yeah, I know what you mean. I've experienced the same thing. I'm not sure why he's such a twat when we're all together. Was Katrina with them?'

'Aye, she was. She's a bonny looking girl. In fact, I'd returned from the shops and when I walked in, it was Katrina who I first saw in the kitchen. I thought it was you and Fiona who were visiting.'

'Why?' he questions.

I stop walking and turn to him. 'I thought it was your Mary. The resemblance is uncanny.'

He holds a deadpan expression. 'Hmm... it's strange. I don't see it. I see a bit of Gillian in her. Katrina will change as she gets older.'

We walk again. 'Gillian was asking how you were,' I say.

'That's nice.'

'What I mean is she was *really* asking about you. It wasn't simply polite conversation.'

'What are you getting at, Geordie?' he says, pulling out a cigarette and sparking up.

'It's obvious to everyone apart from Flaky. She shines a light for you.' The walking halts again as he stares at me.

'The love that dare not speak its name,' he murmurs. 'I am aware of it, but what can I do? I don't encourage or court it. I'm sure it's a passing phase.'

'A passing phase? It's been going on for nearly six years. Is Fiona aware of it?'

'Don't know. Maybe.'

'What? You mean you haven't discussed it with her?'

'Discussed what? That one of her friends, our friends, has the hots for me? That my daughter and Flaky's daughter share a passing resemblance? No! I haven't discussed it with her because there's nothing to discuss. She's never brought it up and neither have I.'

'Passing resemblance? They could almost be sisters.'

He takes an almighty drag on his cigarette as his eyes narrow, glaring at me.

'Maybe Flaky is the father of Mary. Maybe he had it away with Fiona. Have you thought about that?'

'Don't talk daft, man! We're talking about Flaky, the God fearing, devout pescatarian. If he accidentally parks on a double-yellow line, he flagellates himself.'

'I know what you're getting at, Geordie. And the answer is no; Katrina is not my child.'

I drop the subject.

⟶⟩⟩⟩ ⟨⟨⟨⟵

We eat lunch at the windbreak on top of the summit. My sadness and malaise return. There's not much conversation between us. The distant bleating of sheep and the languid buzz of bees are the only sounds to test the silence. A hazy, mellow yellow sun gazes down on us against the backdrop of a dazzling turquoise sky. In the distance is the sparkling glint of the North Sea.

Billy packs away the flask and sandwich box, then zips up his backpack. He stands and surveys the glorious panorama as though it were his very own kingdom. I suppose it is, in a way.

'This place is good for the soul,' he says gently and quietly. 'It doesn't matter what time of year I come here or what the weather is like. It's a steroid shot. An oasis in a desert of white noise.'

'Aye, it has a certain charm. Although, I still deny it's a mountain.'

He smiles and slaps me on the back. 'Let's cut the bullshit. We've known each other too long.'

'What do you mean?'

He slings the backpack on and tightens the straps. 'What's it all about, Geordie?'

'It's Jackie.'

'Go on.'

I feel vulnerable, as though telling my best mate my innermost thoughts is a sign of weakness. But here goes.

'I think she's cheating on me.'

'No way!'

'I'm afraid so. Has Fiona mentioned anything to you about it? She and Jackie are good mates and are always on the phone with each other.'

He stares at the ground thoughtfully and shakes his head from side to side. 'No, nothing.'

'You would tell me if you knew something, right?'

'Geordie, trust me. If Fiona had told me anything, then I'd definitely tell you. You must be wrong. I can't believe it. I know she can give you a tough time, but the way she gazes at you when you're not looking... it's plain to see.'

'What is?'

'She adores you. Anyway, how do you know she's doing the dirty on you?'

As we amble down the pike, treading on soft springy grass, I relate my tale of taking the boys to the park and bumping into Carly. He listens without interrupting until I've finished my sorry saga.

'No matter which way I look at it, she lied to me. It can only mean one thing... she's got herself another fella.'

'Hang on, big boy, back up a bit. Telling a lie doesn't automatically mean she's having a fling. There could be many reasons for not telling the truth.'

'Oh, aye? Such as?'

He stops and rubs at his chin. 'Maybe she's doing something she thinks you wouldn't approve of.'

'She'd be right!'

'I don't mean that. Maybe she's taken up kickboxing or water polo or something.'

'Don't talk wet! You know Jackie. She's bloody headstrong and a rabid feminist. If she wanted to do something, she'd do it whether I approved or not. No, it's over, Bill. I cannae see any way out of this. My life is fucked... again. It's taken me a while to come to terms with being a father and a husband. I had to readjust. It's no longer all about me. It's about my wife and my boys. These last few years have been the happiest of my life, and now it's over. Happiness is not meant for people like me.'

He grabs me by the shirt and jabs a finger at me. 'Stop it right now!' he yells.

'Stop what?' I ask in all innocence.

'Your maudlin bullshit and feeling sorry for yourself! It doesn't suit you, and it solves nothing. Now, listen to me. I can't offer any explanation. But I know this—Jackie would never cheat on you. It goes against everything she stands for. Like you said, she's headstrong. If she wanted to be with another man, she'd end your relationship first, then find a fella. She's not the secretive, undercover type. I'm telling you, Geordie, there has to be a rational explanation for this. We've got to find out what. Hang on, I know. I could ask Fiona to ring her and see what's going on?'

I'm appalled at the idea 'No, for God's sake, don't do that!'

'Why not?'

'Because it completely belittles and undermines me.'

'Okay, why don't you simply ask her? Face to face?'

'Because...'

'Because what?'

'I fear what her answer will be. I'm delaying the inevitable, buying time. I've built a prison of misery, but a prison I'm content to live in at the moment.' I slump to the ground and hold my head in my hands.

He sits down next to me. 'Hey, come on, big man, don't throw the towel in. Let's think of some positive steps we can take.'

Silence visits us once more. After a few minutes of calm reflection, he jumps to his feet.

'I have a plan.'

I brighten slightly. Bill's plans are always good... usually. 'Go on?' I say.

'Is she still taking every Tuesday off to do her own thing?'

'Yes.'

'We'll follow her and find out what she's really up to. I can guarantee it will be something innocent, like flower arranging or boot scooting. Although, I'm not sure line-dancing to country music is innocent. It's the work of the devil and should be made illegal,' he says with a grin.

'No, that's a terrible idea. If she spotted us, it would make things even worse. She'd think I didn't trust her.'

'You don't!'

'Of course, I do, I mean... Christ, I don't know what I think anymore.'

'Listen to me. We'll put on disguises so fiendishly brilliant we won't even recognise each other.'

'Go on?'

'I'll drive up to your place next Monday. You can tell her I fancy a change of scenery to get the creative juices flowing. On Monday night, I'll pretend to receive a call from a guy in Newcastle. I'll say he wants a meeting to discuss a documentary on the band the following day. Ask your mother-in-law to come and babysit for a few hours. We wait until Jackie leaves the house, then we don our disguises and follow her.'

'How are we going to do that with the mother-in-law in the house? Oh, wait, the boys have a swimming lesson next Tuesday morning at nine. I can get her to take them.'

'Perfect. What time does Jackie usually leave?'

'About nine-thirty.'

'I love it when a plan comes together.'

'Where am I going to get a disguise from?'

'Trawl around the second-hand shops or go to one of those places that hire out party costumes. Make sure you're unrecognisable. Although, with that great big noggin of yours, it's going to be pretty hard to do. Make sure you get a good wig.'

'You know what? I believe it could work,' I say with a smile. 'But there's only one problem with your master plan.'

'What?'

'If we follow her, and she is up to no good... then what?'

'Stop being negative. We'll cross that imaginary bridge when, and if, we come to it. Anyway, better to find the truth than live in a state of misery indefinitely.'

'You're right, thanks, Billy Boy. It's time for the truth—for better or for worse.'

'Come on, let's lift our pace. I could murder a couple of pints.'

'Aye, me too. I feel like a weight has been lifted from my shoulders. Action is always better than inaction. Seize the day!'

'That's the spirit!'

'Your shout?'

'No. My advice doesn't come cheap. It's your shout.'

'Fair enough.'

'By the way, I got a call from John Peterson yesterday, and guess what?'

'What?'

'We have a meeting lined up with Jerry Bloomberg, the executive producer of I Will Survive.'

'Brilliant!'

'No, it's not brilliant! It's a nightmare. Be careful what you wish for, Geordie, because it might just happen.'

Chapter Eleven

Operation Stealth – Will's Masterplan

'Geordie, how long have we got?' I ask, staring out of the kitchen window as Jackie strides purposefully along the street away from the house.

'About ten minutes. Her first stop is Kosta's Koffee shop, that's coffee with a K. She'll pop in there to pick up a fancy-schmancy café latte. Four quid a bloody pop!' Geordie replies.

I stare at the side of his massive melon as he squints out the window.

'And there speaks the renaissance man. A guy who thinks it's pretentious to buy a decent cup of coffee. How long does it take her to get coffee?'

'Depends. If she gets a takeaway, then five minutes. If she sits in, she could be there for twenty minutes or more.'

'Right, time to launch Operation Stealth.'

I scoot out of the kitchen and race up the stairs to the second floor, enter the guest bedroom, and retrieve my suitcase from the wardrobe. I peel away the backing tape from the moustache. Standing in front of the mirror, I carefully affix it to my top lip. It looks good—grey and bushy. Next, I attach the eyebrows, again grey and bushy. I dab my face with talcum powder to give myself a pale, washed-out complexion, then carefully position the ashen coloured wig into position and pop on a pair of spectacles with plain glass lenses. To finish it, I slip into an old beige coat bought from a second-hand shop. I deliberately spilt some tea on it to create an authentic doddering old man look. The entire process takes less than two minutes. I shoot back down the stairs, pleased with my disguise.

'What do you think?' I say as I pirouette next to Geordie, who is busily applying his own disguise in the hallway mirror.

He grins. 'Jeez, Billy Boy! You look amazing. Old age suits you. What do you think of mine?'

I focus on him for the first time as my heart sinks. He's wearing an afro wig much akin to the Jackson 5 style of the early seventies. A coloured poncho, knitted in a wash of blazing colours, hangs from his broad shoulders.

'Fuck me sideways,' I whisper.

'You like it?' he asks, pleased with himself.

I stare at the tiled floor for a second as I gather my thoughts.

'Do you know what the first and most important rule of disguise is? To blend into your environment. To be invisible.'

He snorts derisively. 'No, it's not. It's to be unrecognisable, and I think I've pulled it off with some aplomb,' he replies with a hefty dose of pride.

'You resemble a giant bog brush auditioning for Joseph and the Amazing Technicolour Dreamcoat. If you walk down the street like that, you're going to end up with about a hundred kids following you around asking where the circus is.'

'Oh, piss off! There's no pleasing you sometimes. Hang on, I haven't finished yet.'

He pulls a false nose from his pocket and clamps it onto his already oversized hooter.

'Wow! That makes all the difference. It's the little things that count. No one will give you a second glance now.'

He smiles, as though I actually meant it. 'Wait, one more touch, to complete the look.'

A pair of large, round spectacles are balanced precariously on his grotesque nose.

'Come on, we better go,' I say, as I sense Operation Stealth may have already gone tits up.

'Hang on a mo, I have one more thing.'

He turns and walks slap-bang into the wall.

'Damn it!' he yells as his prosthetic nose falls to the ground, followed by his glasses.

I pick up the spectacles and try them on, instantly feeling nauseous and disorientated. Everything is a complete blur. I pull them from my face and hand them back.

'Bloody hell! That's like having a bad acid trip.'

He fumbles under his poncho then hands me a radio. 'Here we go. A pair of walkie talkies with a range of twenty miles.'

I stare at it in disbelief. 'Unlike a mobile phone which has a range of thirteen-thousand miles.'

'You know, you can be extremely negative at times. This lot cost me thirty knicker.'

'State-of-the-art, then?'

'To talk, you need to push the PTT button, here,' he says, demonstrating the bleeding obvious. 'When you've finished talking, you release the button.'

'I know how to use a radio. Come on, let's go.'

We bustle our way to the front door.

'Wait... what's your handle?' he says, looking slightly to the left of me through his Hubble Telescope spectacles.

'What?'

'Your handle. Your code name?'

'Call me Will, or Bill or Billy Boy... whatever,' I wearily sigh.

He grimaces and shakes his head. 'No, no, that won't do at all. We're undercover. No real names.'

I throw my hands in the air. 'I don't know! Call me vexed or something.'

'Vexed it is then.'

'What's your codename?'

'O'Toole.'

'Of course it is.'

'After the actor, Peter O'Toole. I watched a film he was in the other night.'

'How illuminating.'

He closes the door behind us, and we scamper down the steps. I open the boot of my car and pull out a Zimmer frame.

Geordie smiles. 'Nice work. You really look like an old git, now.'

'It's called method acting. Immerse yourself in the part. I have to look, think, and feel like an eighty-year-old man.'

He nods in agreement as I pull out a hearing aid and attach the earpiece.

'What's that for?' he asks, puzzled.

'It's a hearing aid.'

'You didn't tell me you were having trouble with your hearing.'

'I'm not, you plonker! It's part of the disguise.'

'Oh, I see,' he says, rubbing his chin. 'Right, here's the plan; I'll traverse the opposite footpath in a southerly direction, and you take this footpath and traverse...'

'In a southerly direction?'

'Aye, you read my mind. When one of us has an eyeball on the suspect, we call in our position on the walkie-talkie.'

'The suspect. You mean Jackie?'

'I've told you before, no real names. She's the suspect. That's how you must refer to her.'

'I see you've still got an open mind about your wife's mysterious behaviour. That's good to see.'

'Listen Bill, I have a nose for these things,' he says, tapping his bulbous proboscis.

'You certainly do.'

'Come on, we've already lost enough time with your ineptitude.' He glances at his watch. 'It's precisely 10:04 and 25 seconds... approximately. Let Operation Stealth commence.'

He spins around and bangs into the Zimmer frame, sending it tumbling.

'Geordie, take the glasses off. You're going to get yourself mowed down if you insist on wearing them.'

For once, he does what I ask before he strides across the road. I steady myself on the Zimmer frame and shuffle along on the opposite pavement. After less than thirty seconds, he is way ahead of me and if it weren't for the glare of colours shimmering in the sunlight and the giant afro wig bobbing along, I'd have lost sight of him. My walkie-talkie is clipped to the inside of my coat. I stop and press the PTT button.

'Geordie, slow down. I can't keep up,' I hiss.

There's a moment's silence, followed by a crackle from the radio. 'There's no one here called Geordie. Maintain radio etiquette. Over and out.'

'Sorry, come in, O'Toole, come in O'Toole.'

'Roger. Receiving you loud and clear. O'Toole here. Please identify yourself.'

Give me strength! 'Who the hell do you think it is? It's me, Will... erm... Vexed!'

'Roger, Vexed. State your position. Out.'

'About two hundred yards behind you! I'm in character. I can't keep up with your pace. Slow down. Do I make myself clear?'

'Ten-four, Vexed. You're supposed to say—out—after you've finished radio contact. That way, I know you've finished speaking. Out.'

'OUT!'

'Roger, Vexed. No need to get shitty. Out.'

'Did you hear what I said? Out.'

'Roger, ten-four. Request to slow down received loud and clear. Appropriate steps are being taken. Over and out.'

I sluggishly make my way down the street, crossing side roads at pedestrian crossings. After ten minutes, I'm standing outside Kosta's Koffee House. Geordie is nowhere to be seen. There's a small menu in the shop window which I pretend to read, but surreptitiously I scan the occupants inside the shop. There's no sign of Jackie. I speak into my coat.

'Come in, O'Toole. Vexed calling,' I whisper.

'Roger, Vexed. Out.'

'Outside Kosta's Koffee, with a K. No sign of Jac... erm, suspect. Out.'

'Ten-four. Maintain radio silence, Vexed. Out.'

'Why? Have you seen her? Out.'

'No. I'm popping into the bakery. Out'

'What? Out.'

'I'm feeling peckish, and they do the best sausage rolls in the city. Plus, their mushroom soup is to die for. Out.'

'Listen to me, Geordie, you knob-womble, don't you dare...'

There's a click from the walkie-talkie followed by deathly silence. Damn it! This was supposed to be a joint operation. Once again it looks like muggins here, has to take up the slack. A businessman nearly knocks me off my feet as he stumbles out of the door clutching a takeaway coffee and a muffin.

'Hey! Watch where you're going, grandad!' he shouts in a sneering manner. 'Shouldn't you be in a wheelchair with a picnic blanket over you, feeding the ducks in the park instead of clogging up the pavement?'

'Listen, twat-face, if I were twenty-years older I'd knock your bloody head off!'

He laughs at me. 'Yeah, right on... old man. You mean twenty years younger. Dementia is such a shame... isn't it?' he guffaws.

I lift the Zimmer frame and give him a vicious jab to the chest with one of the legs. He looks shocked, surprised, aggrieved and any other adjectives you can throw at him. I feel I may have deviated slightly from my method acting philosophy. The man departs quickly as static buzz from the radio arrests my attention.

'Calling Vexed. Come in, Vexed. O'Toole here. Out.'

'Roger, O'Toole. Out.'

'State your position, Vexed. Out.'

'Pissed off, angry, wondering where I went wrong with my life. Out.'

'Sorry, Vexed. You're breaking up...'

'Yeah, you're not wrong. Out.'

'Repeat, state your position. Out.'

I glance down the high-street and in the distance spot a six-and-a-half-foot man wearing a giant afro wig, and a garish poncho, heading my way.

'Look directly ahead—about forty yards. That's my position. Out.'

'Roger, Vexed. I have an eyeball on you. ETA, about fifty seconds, give or take. Oh, for fuck's sake! Out.'

'What's the matter, O'Toole? Out.'

'My false nose has dropped into my mushroom soup. Out.'

I chuckle to myself. 'Roger that, O'Toole. You always were a fun guy. Out.'

'Not appreciated, Vexed. My marriage is on the line here, and you're making crap jokes.'

'Out?'

'OUT!'

He approaches with the stealth and grace of a bull elephant on Viagra during mating season. Every single person he passes stops and stares at him. I focus my attention back on the coffee shop. The door opens and out she walks. In one hand, her mobile phone, eyes transfixed, in the other hand, a cup of coffee. She bumps into me and automatically apologises. This is the moment of truth. Time for the finest display of acting since Clark Gable said, "Frankly, my dear…"

'I'm so sorry. It's my fault. I was too busy looking at my phone,' she offers by way of explanation.

I pride myself on being a master of dialect and adopt a highland accent.

'Och aye the noo. Nay, werry, wee lassie,' I say, smiling at her benevolently.

'Oh, you must be from Birmingham. I went to university there. Wait… hang on a minute… do we know each other? You look familiar. You weren't a professor there, were you?'

'No, no, no. I'm no professor. I used to be a…'

I struggle to find a past occupation for myself.

'A what?'

'A hedgehog farmer,' I blurt out.

Why did I say that? Why couldn't I have said I was a builder or a taxi driver?

Her eyes narrow. 'A hedgehog farmer?' she probes with disbelief.

'Aye, wee lassie. A hedgehog farmer in Budapest.'

My mind has turned to mush.

'What part of the hedgehog could you possibly utilise?'

Good fucking question… and one I don't readily have an answer for. Come on mate, method acting. I'm Robert De Niro, Al Pacino, and Mr Bean, all rolled into one. I can pull this off.

'It's their quills. They're valuable.'

She appears appalled at the news. 'You're not telling me you kill poor little hedgehogs to use their quills?'

'No, we don't kill them. We harvest the spines. We pluck one or two a week.'

'Do they grow back?'

'Yes. It's like plucking an eyebrow.'

A blinding flash of clarity and reflection hits me. If someone had told me that one day I'd be standing in the middle of a Scottish high-street, dressed as an eighty-year-old man, talking to my best friend's wife—who doesn't recognise me—about how to harvest hedgehog quills, then I would have said they were mad. Funny how life turns out.

'What are they used for... the spines?'

She's an inquisitive bugger. I'll give her that. 'Brushes.'

'Like hairbrushes?'

'Sort of. Extremely popular with the Arabs. They use them to brush camels' tails. Camel racing is a big sport in the Middle East. They treat them like we treat thoroughbred racehorses.'

'Well, I never,' she gushes.

My sentiments entirely.

'And why Budapest?'

I have no idea why.

'Not many people know this, but Budapest is the international hub for hedgehog quill auctions.'

She looks more confused than I do, and that's saying something.

'Was it a lucrative business?'

Give me strength! Hasn't she got anything better to do?

'It was until the bottom fell out of it, the market, not the hedgehogs. Anyway, to be honest with you, I didn't enjoy flying back and forth to the Middle East. The heat was too much for me.'

She giggles. 'You should write a book about it. You could call it Prickly Heat! Ha, ha, get it?' she cackles loudly, then slaps me so hard on the front of my shoulder I nearly topple from my Zimmer frame.

'Oh, I'm sorry! I didn't mean to hit you that hard,' she says with a look of concern. 'My husband always says I don't know my own strength.'

Talking of her husband, here comes the big dolt now. I stare over her shoulder at him. We lock eyes. I raise my eyebrows and shake my head slightly. His gaze falls upon his wife, who has noticed that I'm looking at something or someone behind her. As she turns to take a glance, Geordie hops into a butcher's shop. I feel my moustache slip and have to use my bottom lip to hold it in place. Jackie returns her perplexed gaze back onto me.

'Thanks for the chat. It was interesting,' she says. 'What's your name if you don't mind me asking?'

For God's sake, woman! Go, please, I beg you!

I manage to open one side of my mouth slightly while keeping the moustache in place.

'Bob,' I drawl, sounding like someone who's recently suffered a massive stroke.

'Sorry?'

'Bob,' I repeat, with one side of my face completely paralysed.

'Bob?' she says.

My eyes light up, and I nod enthusiastically. A crease appears on her forehead. She isn't sure about me, which isn't surprising as I'm not sure about myself anymore. A few tense moments pass as my bottom lip develops an excruciating cramp. Eventually, her genial smile returns.

'I'm Jackie, Bob. Take care.'

At last, she buggers off! I quickly reattach the moustache as a trickle of sweat inches down my spine. Geordie's big melon pops out from the butcher's doorway. He's less than five feet away but insists on speaking into the radio.

'O'Toole here. Come in, Vexed. Out.'

'Vexed, here. Out.'

'Is the coast clear? Out.'

'Yes, O'Toole. I can confirm the suspect has decamped from the immediate vicinity. Out.'

He walks from the doorway, munching on a sausage roll.

'Where is she?'

'Headed that way,' I say, pointing down the street, noticing that Jackie has lifted her pace and is quickly disappearing from view into the melee of shoppers. 'Come on, we're going to lose her if we're not careful.'

I shuffle off, clutching the Zimmer frame while Geordie surges ahead. Within minutes, I've not only lost sight of Jackie but also of her gormless husband. I take five minutes before I eventually catch up to him as he emerges from another bakery chomping on a chocolate éclair.

'What took you so long?' he asks as a blob of cream attaches itself to the end of his gargantuan hooter.

'I'm on a Zimmer. It may arouse suspicion if I was zooming along like Usain Bolt.'

I peer around the corner and spot Jackie at the far end of the street, a good two hundred yards away. She takes a left and disappears from view.

'Shit! Come on, she's turned down the next street,' I urge.

I lift my pace trying to keep up with Geordie as he hurtles along. People instinctively give us a wide birth as we approach... I'm not sure why. As we progress down the street, the shops thin out, replaced by townhouses. I'm breathing hard and sweating profusely. My left eyebrow comes loose, momentarily obscuring my eye. It gives up the will to live and slides down my cheek, then drops to the ground. We come to the end of the road and stop to catch our breath. The street is lined with well-to-do Georgian townhouses, much akin to Geordie's pad. On the opposite side is an extensive park, with trees, benches, and a children's playground in the distance.

'I don't like the smell of this,' Geordie laments.

'No. And I don't particularly like the smell of you. Let's cross over to the park and follow from that side.'

Geordie scampers across the road as I grip the Zimmer and lurch and pivot like Quasimodo on a pogo stick, as I try to keep up with him. I'm regretting the Zimmer frame idea as I am my attire. It's a fairly warm day, by Scottish standards, and the wig, long overcoat, and relentless pace are taking their toll.

We trail her for another fifty yards before she abruptly stops, opens a gate and walks into the garden of a townhouse.

We take up position on a park bench opposite. Geordie sticks his hand under his poncho, pulls out a rolled-up newspaper, unfurls it, then fumbles his spectacles onto his nose.

'That's better. It's like looking through binoculars.'

Jackie jauntily sidles up the garden path, climbs a set of steps and raps on a large green door, which is immediately flung open. A shortish man, about mid-thirties, splays his arms out theatrically. Words are exchanged, but we are too far away to decipher them. They exchange faux kisses to either cheek. The man does a quick scan of the horizon and for one heart-stopping moment his eyes rest on us. Our deception could be foiled. He frowns for a moment before he ushers Jackie inside and closes the door.

'That's that then. It's the end of my marriage. My worst fears have come to fruition,' Geordie mumbles sorrowfully.

He may have a point.

Chapter Twelve

Busted - Will's Masterplan

'I've seen it with my own eyes. The die is cast. What's been done cannot be undone. She's cheating on me. It's as plain as the nose on my face.'

I stare at his schnozzle which is anything but plain. 'Get a grip, man. The guy is obviously gay. You could tell by his mannerisms. The way they greeted, the way they kissed, the way he delicately touched her shoulder as he corralled her into the house. If he was her lover, he'd have either kissed her on the lips or quickly pulled her inside.'

I notice another man heading our way on the opposite side of the street. Again, mid-thirties, average build, a handsome man with a stylish dress sense.

'Oh, and you're an expert on gay men, are you?'

'No. But if a man is from the camp, camp, it's obvious.'

'The camp, camp?'

'Yes, you know... when they show affectations of being gay. Over--exaggerated enthusiasm; arms and hands with a life of their own; the slightly high-pitched voice and the constant use of the word darling.'

'You don't half speak shite, sometimes!'

The man striding along opposite takes a right turn into the same garden, mounts the steps, knocks on the door then lets himself in.

'Fuck me blue!' Geordie cries. 'She's not happy with just the one.'

'Let's not jump to any conclusions yet,' I advise.

'And was he gay?'

'No. He was definitely not gay. Could be bi, though.'

'So, my loving wife is having an illicit affair with a homosexual and a bisexual. What next? Maybe throw in a Lady-Boy for good measure. In for a penny, in for a pound! It's over, Bill. It's over.'

'I admit, it's not looking good at the moment, but we still know nothing. It could all be innocent. Let's see how it plays out.'

He lifts his poncho, sticks his hand down the front of his trousers, retrieves a brown paper bag, and pulls out a large pork pie. I peer at him in disgust. He takes a giant bite and munches away with little enthusiasm. He holds the pie out in my direction.

'Wanna bite?'

'Thanks for the offer, but I'll give it a miss. I'm trying to give up pubic hair.'

He takes another bite. I hear voices from behind. Two joggers dart past us. One is tall and wiry, the other stocky and muscular. They're laughing and joking as they race across the road and straight into the garden opposite. Up the steps they go. One loud rap and they let themselves in, as well. Remnants of the pork pie fall to the pavement.

'Explain that?' he murmurs. 'The woman's a brazen harlot. I've heard of threesomes, but a fivesome is taking the fucking biscuit.'

I'm as confused as he is.

'She'll not get the kids. I'll fight her all the way. She can have the house, alimony, the car, whatever she wants, but she'll not take my lads off me!'

'The vast majority of custody battles always favour the mother. And with your chequered past, you've no chance.'

'Thanks pal! You're always a source of comfort.'

'That's what mates are for,' I say, patting his leg.

My moustache falls into my lap as I notice a police car slowly heading in our direction. It glides past and rolls on down the road. Red brake lights appear as it comes to a stop. It's followed by a high-pitched whine as it reverses back up the road, stopping directly in front of us. The driver's window retracts and two dopey looking police officers peer out.

'Hey, Geordie, we thought it was you!' shouts the copper behind the wheel, beaming broadly.

Geordie looks up from his paper and smiles sheepishly.

'Constable Dankworth, how yer going?'

The copper in the passenger seat leans across and waves. 'Hi, Geordie,' he says, accompanied by a gormless grin.

'Constable Constable, good to see you.'

'What's with the outfit?'

'It's a surprise for the boys. You know, a bit of dress up fun.'

Both coppers nod, smiling.

'Who's the old man?' Constable Dankworth asks, studying me.

'He's... uh... he's my grandad,' he says without conviction.

'You said your grandad was dead?' he questions suspiciously.

'This is the other one. I'm entitled to two, you know.'

'Why has he only got one eyebrow?' Constable Constable asks.

Geordie stares at me.

'Alopecia. He suffers from stress and incontinence. What are you two up to?' he says, changing the conversation.

'We've had reports about two shady looking characters acting suspiciously. We're doing a few circuits to see if we can spot them.'

'Do you have a description?' Geordie asks.

'Yeah, but it's vague. Some guy wearing a garish coloured shawl of some sort and sporting a Busby hat. Tall, probably about your height. The other guy is older, grey coat, bushy moustache. Apparently, he can move pretty fast on a Zimmer frame. You haven't seen either of them, have you?'

'No, can't say that I have. Have you noticed anything, grandad?'

'No, son. But my eyes aren't what they used to be,' I reply in a brittle voice as I rest my arms over the Zimmer frame.

'One of them goes by the name O'Toole and the other is called Vexed or something like that,' Constable Dankworth continues.

'How do you know?' Geordie enquires.

'Their walkie talkies keep cutting in and out of the police waveband. Must be some cheap crap they're using.'

Geordie and I exchange glances.

'I think they're engaged in a reconnaissance mission. You know, casing a joint, probably a bank.'

Constable Constable leans further across. 'When the blag goes down, we'll be waiting for them, won't we, Constable Dankworth?'

'Too right, Constable Constable. There's not much gets past us.'

There's an awkward silence as we all eyeball each other. Their police radio crackles into life.

'Charlie 1 to Lemming 2. Come in. Over.'

'Lemming 2. Over.'

'Attempted break in at 16 Potterton Way, Newington. Suspects are still in the vicinity. Proceed ASAP. Over.'

'Copy that Charlie 1. On our way. Over. This could be our suspects now.'

Constable Dankworth hits the siren, and the car screeches off down the road. Its brake lights suddenly flash red, accompanied by a squeal of tyres. It does a slow, meticulous, three-point turn before flying past us.

Constable Constable leans out of the window and shouts. 'Geordie, you still on for darts, tomorrow night?'

Geordie lifts a finger in the air and gives a nod. The patrol car comes to a shuddering halt as it stops at a zebra crossing a hundred yards up the road. A gaggle of pedestrians amble slowly across, before it takes off again at an alarming speed. The car disappears from view as its siren fades.

'Fuckwits,' Geordie mumbles. 'They couldnae catch a dose of the clap.'

'That's why I sleep easy on a night, knowing the thin blue line is out there protecting us. Come on, our work here is done. Let's head home.'

As we pass a builder's skip outside a house, we remove our disguises and drop them in the bin, along with the Zimmer frame.

'What do you want to do with the walkie talkies?' I ask.

'Keep them. I'll give them to the boys.'

'Okay, but remember to change the frequency, otherwise you'll have a SWAT team crashing through the window in the middle of the night.'

⤜⤜⤜ ⤛⤛⤛

Wallace and Bobby hop down from the table, dash across the room, and pull out a box of toys from under a small side table. I pick up their plates and stack them in the dishwasher. Geordie pulls two beers from the fridge, cracks the tops and hands me one. He takes two large gulps, nearly emptying the bottle. As I set the table for the adults, the front door bangs shut as Jackie calls out.

'It's only me. I'm home!'

Geordie glances at the clock on the wall—5:10 pm.

'The return of The Scarlet Woman of Scotland,' he growls under his breath.

'Hey, remember what we talked about? Keep calm, act as if nothing's wrong,' I remind him.

'Aye. Don't you worry about me. I'm a master of the long game,' he says.

Jackie bustles into the kitchen carrying an assortment of bags. She's all smiles and looks radiant.

'Ooh, something smells good. What's for dinner?' she asks.

'Cauliflower cheese and crusty fresh bread,' snarls the master of the long game.

'What's wrong with you, Captain Grumpy?' she says, as she drops her bags onto the couch and kicks her shoes off.

I offer her a warm smile. 'The trip to Newcastle to see the documentary maker was a waste of time. We must have got our wires crossed. We thought he wanted to do a rockumentary on the history of the band.'

'And he didn't?'

'Nah, he wanted to send a film crew with us when we do our next world tour. I told him we don't do world tours anymore. Then, when we got back here, the musical juices weren't flowing. Overall, it's been a waste of a day,' I lie. 'That's the thing with writing songs. Some days it's there and other days it isn't. It's the nature of the beast.'

'If it were easy, everyone would do it,' she replies. 'Hello boys,' she calls out to her sons.

'Hello, mummy,' they reply in unison.

'Where's mother?' she asks Geordie.

'In her room, taking a nap.'

I pull a bottle of wine from the fridge. 'Can I get you a glass of wine, Jackie?'

'Yes please, thanks, Will.'

I fill a glass and hand it to her as she sits down at the table.

'What sort of day have you had?' Geordie asks

She takes a genteel sip of wine and throws her hair back.

'I've had a lovely day. I've just been for a long workout.'

'Where at?' he hisses.

'At the gym, of course. Where else would I go? Oh, I bumped into a really interesting old man this morning and had the weirdest conversation.'

'Really?' Geordie says, glancing at me.

'Yes, he had the strangest accent. It was sort of Brummie interspersed with bits of Scottish.'

I cough. 'Maybe he was born in the midlands but lived in Scotland for a while. Accents can get mangled, sometimes,' I offer.

'Hmm... maybe. At one point he said och aye the noo, for God's sake. I've lived my entire life in Scotland, and I've never heard anyone use that expression. The only time you hear it is when you're watching old black and white films set in Scotland, made by English people. Anyway, he used to make a living selling hedgehog quills to the Arabs—apparently.'

'Is that so?' Geordie says, raising an eyebrow in my direction. 'Sounds a little unlikely.'

'He was based in Budapest. He said it was the international trading centre for buying and selling hedgehog quills. His main customers were the Arabs who make brushes out of them for camel's tails.'

'The guy sounds like a complete fruit loop,' Geordie sneers. 'Hedgehog quill auctions indeed. He obviously needs looking after.'

'Hmm... there was something not quite right about him, but I couldn't put my finger on it. He definitely looked familiar. Oh, and there was another guy, who I didn't see, who was wandering around wearing a Busby and a colourful blanket. He kept muttering to himself, constantly repeating his name, Roger O'Toole. I bumped into loads of people who were talking about him.'

'You know what they say, O'Toole by name, O'Toole by nature. Probably a hapless, barmy vagrant who has lost his marbles,' I say, staring back at Geordie.

'Maybe. So, quite an eventful day, really.'

She stands up and lets out a little groan.

'What's wrong?' Geordie asks

'My legs are like jelly. I think I may have overdone the squats.'

Geordie and I exchange furtive glances. She takes another sip of wine and grimaces.

'Oh no, my throat's feeling sore. I hope I'm not coming down with a bug.'

Geordie's face is like thunder. I quickly pull another beer from the fridge and hand it to him.

'Here you go, big fella. Why don't you go outside and take in some fresh air for a while? I'll sort dinner out.'

He wanders into the back garden and sits on a bench, staring into the distance.

'He can be such a moody bugger some days,' Jackie moans as she tops up her glass. 'It isn't anything to do with me taking Tuesdays off, is it? Has he said anything to you?'

'No, nothing. And believe me, if it bothered him, I'd have been the first to get a blast in the ears. I told you, it's the music. He's such a perfectionist. If we have a difficult day, he gets in a right mood. Leave him be and he'll come good.'

She smiles at me. 'Yeah, you're right. You'd think I'd be used to him by now.'

'Believe me, you never get used to Geordie.'

She laughs and saunters over to the boys. 'What have my two little men been up to all day?'

Chapter Thirteen

Question, Answer, Solution?

As I cycle along leafy streets, a soft summer breeze brushes my face with the sweet scent of cherry blossom. I'm nearing my destination and the butterflies in my stomach are stirring. It's my third session with Dr Engle, and I've got to admit, last week's primal therapy was traumatic. It rekindled painful memories and emotions. My sleep and mood were subsequently affected. A malaise swamped me. I'd become distant, absorbed, troubled. Sometimes, when alone, I find myself crying like a bairn for no reason—and I don't do crying. I now understand where my rage stems from, but it hasn't made me feel any better about myself.

I dismount and wheel my bike up the narrow garden path, which has been ambushed either side by budding roses. Clematis droops from a row of trellises straddling the walkway. I feel like an unwanted extra in a period drama as I climb the well-worn steps and press the bell. The electronic chime sounds incongruous to the setting. As I wait, my eyes fell upon the Pentland Hills rising in the east. Measured, padded footsteps progress towards me, accompanied by the outline of Mrs Engle, through the coloured glass mosaic.

'Hello Geordie! Please come in. I see you've ridden here. How long did it take you?'

'A tad over thirty minutes. I took the scenic route. Tried to keep off the main road as much as possible. There are some terrible drivers about.'

She laughs as she guides me down the corridor towards the therapy room.

'Would you care for tea and biscuits?' she asks, knocking twice on the door as she pushes it ajar.

'Aye, that's very kind of you.'

She throws me a warm smile before retracing her steps up the hallway towards the kitchen. I push open the door and enter. Dr Engle is sitting with his back to me at his desk, engrossed in a spreadsheet on his laptop screen.

'Take a seat, Geordie. I'll be with you in a second. I'm trying to get my head around these bloody figures,' he mumbles without looking up.

I collapse into a comfortable modern leather couch, rest one leg across the top of the other, and fidget. After five minutes of silence, Mrs Engle comes bustling through the door carrying a wicker tray containing refreshments.

'For heaven's sake, Jonas! Don't be so rude! You have a client waiting. Now turn the laptop off and attend to your business.'

'Oh, I'm sorry, Joyce. I got so wrapped up in these figures, I forgot.'

'It's not me you should apologise to,' scolds his wife as she pours steaming tea into the cups. 'I'll let you do your own milk and sugar. Geordie, the glass of water is for you. Right, if you need me, Jonas, I'll be in the garden.'

She leaves as her husband pays his gratitude. 'Thank you, dear.'

'Thanks, Mrs Engle,' I call out after her.

Jonas shuts the lid on his laptop and takes up a seat opposite me as he prepares his tea.

He sighs. 'I suppose I should have it black, without sugar. Apparently, it's supposed to be far more beneficial when taken au naturel.'

I grab a ginger nut biscuit and relax into the couch. It emits a comforting, creaky leather moan. As I dunk my biscuit in the tea, I notice Jonas does the same. Our eyes lock on to each other. I grin as he chuckles. After a few seconds, we stick the soggy end into our mouths and chew.

'Dunking is a fine art,' he states.

'It is indeed.'

'Dunk too quickly, and the biscuit is still hard. Dunk too long and you risk it going mushy and dropping off into the bottom of your cup. Nothing worse. Takes years of practice to master it.'

We both sip our tea and study each other. He appears weary compared to our last session. His head turns slightly as he glances wistfully out of the window at the green hills in the distance. Another sigh.

'Time is an odd thing. I can't believe a week has passed since I last saw you. It barely feels like a couple of days. My next book is going to be about time.'

'Really? What's it called?'

'The perception of time.'

'What's it about?' I instantly regret my ridiculous question.

'The perception of time,' he replies, sporting a wry smirk as he peers at me over the rim of his spectacles.

I offer him a sheepish, apologetic wince.

'How have you been?'

I vibrate my lips together and moan. 'Not too good,' I say as I recount my state of mind and troubled sleep.

He listens patiently, occasionally stroking his manicured whiskers. I ramble on for a good ten minutes until I grind to a halt.

'Hmm... I see,' he says as he rises unsteadily from his seat and totters back to his desk

He pulls a large leather-bound notebook from a drawer, groaning as he does so.

'I have a transcript from last week's primal therapy recording. I've also made extensive notes. My work doesn't end the moment you leave the room. I've got to justify my exorbitant prices somehow,' he chuckles.

I offer him a faint smile as he resumes his seat. He adjusts his glasses and flicks through the pages.

'What you've been experiencing is perfectly normal. I expected worse. Your melancholy will disappear with time.'

'I'm not certain it will, doctor. I'm not blaming you, but I think you've opened a door to a cellar which should have remained locked,' I say, wringing my hands together.

'Geordie, believe me, it *will* get better. Day by day, little by little. Think of it like having an operation. You're bound to be battered and bruised when you come out of the anaesthetic. Your therapy last week was the equivalent of a mind operation.'

I tilt my head towards him.

'There are other things preying on my mind. You remember the part where me and Iain crashed into the giant of a man on the stairwell?'

He continues flicking through his pages.

'Yes. I have the notes right here in front of me. You said you were terrified. Initially, the man looked angry. Then he softened and offered you a friendly smile, patted you both on the head and dropped fifty pence each into your hands. What about it? Do you see some significance in the event?'

'Yes. I've replayed the scene over and over in my head and each time it becomes clearer.'

His eyes swivel away from his notes as he gazes at me inquisitively. 'Go on.'

'Apart from him being a giant of a man, he had soft brown eyes. His hands were like anvils. He sported a long, shiny black ponytail which fell below his shoulders. His coat was an olive-green trench coat, you know, like an old army coat from the Great War?'

'They were called Greatcoats. Made from Melton cloth.'

I lift myself slowly from the chair and stand rigid in front of him. 'Imagine me with a ponytail and a long overcoat, and what do you see?'

He removes his spectacles as his mouth falls open. 'Good grief! He was your father!'

⟶⟫⟫ ⟪⟪⟵

I glance at the clock. My hour is nearly up.

'How can a man father two children then abandon them? How can he leave his spouse, who is obviously struggling with drug addiction, to raise the bairns? Why did he never contact me? What had I ever done to deserve that, apart from being born?' My emotions well as I try hard to remain composed.

'The problem is, Geordie, we know nothing of his situation. Maybe he didn't abandon you? Who knows what sort of relationship was happening between him and your mother? And how do you know he never tried to contact you? You said your Nan and Gramps brought you up. Did they ever say anything about your father?'

'I only ever asked about him once. Nan said he'd gone away and wouldn't be coming back.'

'How did you feel at the time?'

'I felt nothing.'

'No sense of loss? No sense of rage?'

I shake my head.

'A lot of orphans concoct a fantasy that one day their mother or father will return to claim them. More often than not, they'll imagine the parent to be super wealthy, or a famous person and they'll ride off into the sunset together and live happily ever after. It's a coping strategy. Have you ever experienced anything similar?'

'No, never.'

He glances at his notes again. 'During our first session, you described your feelings towards your mother as mixed. After her death, not long after your brother's, you said you missed her. As time passed, you had negative feelings towards her, not hatred, but resentment. Given she was probably a drug addict and in a toxic relationship with this so called lodger, Tom Jackson, how do you feel about your mother now?'

I sigh and lean back into the couch. 'Sad, I suppose. She wasn't in control of her situation, but it still doesn't excuse her. As for the scumbag Jackson, I hate him with a passion. If I could get my hands on the bastard, I'd break his neck.'

Probably not the wisest statement I've come out with considering I'm here for anger management.

Doctor Engle peers over his spectacles at me. 'What were your grandparents like?'

'In what way?'

'Were they loving? Did they provide you with a stable environment?'

'Oh, aye. I never missed out on anything, and they weren't wealthy by any means. They sacrificed a lot for me. As for loving... yeah, I guess so.'

'You seem unsure?'

'They were from a different age. They lived through the war and austerity. Their generation didn't outwardly show much affection. I play with my boys and cuddle and kiss them on the cheek. I tell them I love them. But I got little of that from Nan or Gramps. I certainly wasn't unique. Like I say, a different generation.'

'Did they discipline you?'

'Not physically. Nan could have a sharp tongue on her when I did something wrong.'

'She was the disciplinarian, not your grandfather?'

'Yes.'

'Who handles the discipline in your household?'

'Jackie, without a doubt. Again, only verbally. I'm like my Gramps. I'm a big softy with them. They can wrap me around their little finger. Maybe it's compensation because of my childhood.'

'Hmm... maybe. You realise he could still be alive?'

'Who?'

'Your father. He'd only be in his sixties, maybe early seventies. Have you ever thought about tracking him down and meeting with him? It could help.'

I gulp hard. The thought had never occurred to me. 'I don't see how it could help. He left me; I didn't leave him. Why should I give him the possibility of repenting his sins?'

'Forgiveness can be cathartic.'

I'm not sure where he's heading with this line of questioning. I'm here to talk about my anger issues and how to curb them. Picking over rotten fruit isn't achieving anything.

'To be honest, doctor, even if I wanted to find him, which I don't, and even if he were still alive, I wouldn't know where to look for him. The whole point of my coming here was to find a solution to my volatile temper. As interesting as it is to trawl over old events, I can't see how it's going to help me.'

He chuckles. 'You can't find the answer if you don't know the question.'

I'm becoming increasingly exasperated. The last thing I need is cryptic platitudes.

'You're becoming restless, impatient?'

'Aye. I thought I was paying you to supply the answer!'

He smiles benevolently. 'I have the question and I have the answer. I had them both within twenty minutes of meeting you.'

'Then, for Christ's sake, man, tell me what they are!'

He returns his attention to his bloody notebook again, flicking through page after page.

'You recall during our first session I got you to list, in chronological order, all the times you lost your temper in an aggressive manner?'

I exhale in a resigned fashion. 'Yes.'

'I'd like to pick a few instances out and examine them more closely.'

'Okay, if you insist. Fire away,' I say, with little enthusiasm.

'The time you were in a curry house with some of your bandmates. A group of boorish rugby fans entered and abused an Indian waiter. They were calling him racist names and trying to humiliate him.'

'What about it?'

'You stood up for the waiter and that's when the fight occurred.'

'Yes.'

'Why did you stand up for him?'

'Because they were picking on him. It was wrong.'

'There are many things wrong in the world, but you don't fix them all. Why this occurrence?'

'I don't know. It was there, right in my face, I suppose.'

'I want you to close your eyes and reimagine the scene in your head. I want you to smell and taste the food, hear the voices, absorb the atmosphere, envisage the faces.'

I close my eyes and attempt to replay the film in my mind.

'Take as long as you need.'

It takes an age, but ever so slowly, my senses recreate the scene. I can see the rugby lads shouting at the waiter. I can smell beef madras and taste chapatis. The waiter drops a dish. Curry splashes onto the shoe of one of the rugby lads. He tells the waiter to lick it off. My anger burns, slow and purposeful, like a fire being stoked. I tell them to stop. He points his finger at me and hurls abuse. Then it starts... the fight.

I open my eyes.

'Okay, doc, what next?

'Were you back there?'

'Yes.'

'What was the overriding emotion you experienced?'

'Anger.'

'No, no! What emotional response caused your anger?'

'Injustice caused my anger.'

Dr Engle's eyes shine with a burning intensity. He lurches forward and slaps me hard on the thigh.

'That's it, my boy! You have your question; you have your answer; now let's find your solution.'

※ ⟫⟫ ⟪⟪ ※

'Let us talk about anger for a moment. Many people wrongly assume anger is *always* a negative emotion, which undoubtedly it can be. However, it's a very basic emotion. Think of a coin. The coin has two sides, as does anger. There's irrational, violent anger which leads people to perpetrate gross acts of violence based on the flimsiest of reasons, or sometimes for no reason at all. Then there's justified anger.

The defining moment in your life was the late afternoon in Glasgow when you walked out of the cinema as a young boy holding the hand of your younger brother. You crossed the road at the zebra crossing and a drunken, off-duty police officer mowed down your sibling. You experience anger and guilt. Anger towards the driver of the car and guilt for not protecting your younger brother. Your anger was borne from a sense of injustice. You were doing nothing wrong. You followed the rules and crossed at the appropriate place. Your world was suddenly turned upside down. Nothing made sense anymore. In that moment, injustice became your lightning rod, your conduit. Whenever you encountered injustice, you would act. You could not allow the death of Iain to happen again—metaphorically.'

His words spin around inside my head like candy floss around the stick; honeycombed, ephemeral, lacking substance. There's silence until I find my voice.

'All our lives we're told anger and violence are bad; kindness and forgiveness are good.'

He winces as he leans back in his chair. 'What happens when people don't stand up to injustice? Terrible things happen to innocent people. Think of Nazi Germany or any tyranny. Think of bullies, rapists, child abusers, wife-beaters. Without justified anger, there'd be chaos; dog eat dog, survival of the fittest, and damn the rest.'

I contemplate his words.

'Screaming threats into a seven-year-old's face is never defensible. Any other person would have had a quiet word with the lad or his mother. I terrified the wee bairn. If truth be told, I'm ashamed and mortified at my behaviour. It's one thing to give a good hiding to a brute of a man who is picking on someone because of their skin colour, but terrifying the life out of a young lad is never defensible.'

He rubs at his chin and breathes out heavily. 'No, you're right. And that is what we aim to fix.'

'What you and my wife don't understand is my anger is like lightning. It overwhelms me in a matter of seconds. It doesn't allow time for rational thought. One second, I feel myself getting angry—then boom! It explodes.'

His attention returns to the transcript. We appear to be going around in ever diminishing circles.

'Hmm... interesting,' he murmurs. 'There's one incident here which puzzles me. It's from the early days of the band. You were rehearsing and your bandmate, Bill, said something to upset you. You became angry and went for him but stopped yourself. Talk me through the situation.'

'Bill had a new song, and I'd spent hours at home working on a cracking bass line. He didn't like it and was quite dismissive. He said it didn't have the right feeling.'

'What happened next?'

'I threw my bass down and went for him. As quick as a flash, he picked up an empty beer bottle resting on his amp, smashed it, and held it out towards my neck. I paused.'

'Were you scared?'

'No. I could have taken the bottle from him in an instant and given him a slap. But I didn't.'

'Because he'd stood up to you?'

'No. It was because I liked Billy Boy from the moment I first met him. He was the first person who was similar to me... regarding music, I mean. Bill was passionate about it. He lived and breathed it. It felt like at last I belonged. I'd found my...' I close my eyes and rock back and forth.

'Brother?'

I sniff. 'Aye, spiritually, at least. It's why I paused. It gave me a few valuable seconds to assess the situation and realise giving my best pal a bust lip because he didn't like my bass line was over the top.'

'How long did you pause for?'

'I counted to five in my head, then smiled at him. He lowered the bottle, apologised, and said the bass line was great, but not for that song.'

'We found the question. We found the answer. Now we've found the solution,' he says.

I'm baffled. The doctor notices my bewildered expression.

'Don't you see, Geordie... the pause. This is the only incident when you constrained your anger. You did it by counting to five. It was the exact amount of time for emotion to subside and for rational thought take over.'

'Surely it can't be so simple?'

Dr Engle relaxes back into his chair, slams his notebook shut and chortles.

'As humans, we tend to overthink things.'

'That's rich coming from a bloody psychiatrist!'

'Ha, ha! Yes, we are culprits. This is true. Sometimes simple is the best route. Okay, we're finished. This session and your therapy are over.'

He stands and shuffles unsteadily to his desk and deposits his notebook back into the drawer.

'Hang on a minute! You're saying to control my anger, all I need to do is pause? I've already explained; sometimes it explodes. I don't get time to pause, to reflect.'

'No, you don't pause. You count to five, in your head or aloud. The analytical part of your brain performs counting. Anger lies in the emotional side. Cause and effect. Counting is the cause which creates the effect—the pause.'

He returns to his seat and flops down, exhausted. He yawns.

'You can pay Joyce on the way out, and I wish you all the best with everything.'

I shake his hand and meander to the door, not sure what to make of it all. I don't feel like we've achieved anything.

'Thanks for your time, Jonas,' I mumble, pulling open the door.

'You're confused at the moment. It will pass. Be happy in your skin, Geordie—it's a good skin and fits you well.'

His eyes close and his head drops. A gentle, rasping sound escapes from his mouth. As I make my way to the entrance hall, I develop a lump in my throat. I can't remember the last time anyone said something positive about me. Occasionally, even the biggest dolt needs a kind word or two and a pat on the back.

Chapter Fourteen

Highland Fling – Will's Nightmare

'Geordie! For God's sake! Slow down! We're well ahead of schedule. There's no need to break the land speed record,' I beseech, to negligible effect.

'Chill out, Billy Boy. I know these highland roads like the back of my hand,' he replies with a cavernous grin as he turns to me.

'Please do not take your eyes off the road whilst talking to me. There is no need to engage in eye contact with a passenger while you're driving.'

We spent the previous night at Geordie's pad, rose at four and were in the car thirty minutes later as the sun rose. I nodded off on a couple of occasions where the road was long and straight. Alas, with Geordie driving, my sleep had been fitful thanks to constant hypnic jerks as images of cars careering off cliff edges constantly haunted my dreams. It hadn't seemed to bother the other two in the backseats; Robbo gently snored away and occasionally let out a fart. As for Flaky, well at one point I thought he may have expired if it hadn't been for the thin but steady stream of saliva which glacially oozed from the side of his mouth.

'Sat nav says we're only five miles from our destination,' Geordie says as he parks the Range Rover up on the side of the road to take in the lie of the land.

The further we progress into the highlands, the worse the weather becomes. Low cloud and mizzle hang like a fisherman's net over the landscape of sweeping moorland. Gigantic mountains block the horizon, their peaks hidden by dense swathes of cotton wool. Geordie winds the window down and sticks his gargantuan sized head outside and takes in a deep breath in an exaggerated manner.

'Ah! Smell that!' he says with immense pride. 'That is what you call fresh air. The purest air; the air of the highland glens, the air of the...'

'Oh, shut the fuck up, will you? And put your window up. It's bloody freezing. Has this godforsaken wasteland ever seen the sun?' I bark at him.

He fixes me with a mean glare. 'That's sacrilege,' he whispers menacingly. 'How dare you disparage God's own country, you Sassenach heathen. See those mountains over yonder? They're proper mountains. They've earned the right to be called mountains, not like those pustulant carbuncles you have in Yorkshire.'

'Yeah, yeah, whatevs. Come on, let's get going. Next left down a gravel track, according to the sat nav.'

We leave the bitumen and navigate onto a gravel track.

'I can't believe I'm here. What happened?' I lament.

'What do you mean?'

'In the space of a few weeks we've gone from contemplating a hare-brained scheme to signing contracts to take part in a crap reality TV show. And now, a weekend freezing our nuts off on a survival course. It has to be a dream. I'm going to wake up at some point.'

'You know your problem, Bill. You don't like to get out of your comfort zone.'

'Too right, I don't. I like my comfort zone. The whole point of my life is to spend as much time as possible in my comfort zone.'

'You need to broaden your horizons, face new challenges, grab life by the balls and squeeze the crap out of it. Nothing ventured, nothing gained. Once you get into the swing of things, you'll start enjoying yourself.'

'I can assure you, there's no enjoyment in sleeping rough, shitting in a field and living off rabbit droppings.'

As we descend the winding track, the view becomes clearer. To the west is the grey Atlantic Ocean, gently lapping against a beautiful and pristine cove surrounded by undulating sand dunes. To the north are miles of craggy rocks and outcrops dusted with verdant grass. It is breath-taking, but I'm certainly not going to acknowledge it to Geordie.

We dip down into a circular hollow where we spot a flashy motorhome parked next to some picnic tables and a barbecue area. As the Range Rover comes to a halt, Geordie lets out a sigh.

'I'm feeling a little nervous,' he says hesitantly.

'Why?'

He turns to me, embarrassed. 'Well, you know?'

'No... I don't,' I reply, as I undo my seatbelt.

'Hammer Harrington... you know.'

'What about him?' I say, as I stretch and yawn.

'He's a hero of mine. The guy's a legend. He's authentic. If you ever wanted someone in your corner in a tight spot, then Hammer's your man,' he gushes in admiration.

'He might be your man, but he's not mine. The guy's a twat. He's nothing, but a glorified self-promoter whose only purpose in life is to perpetuate the myth he's some real-life superhero. Plus, his father was loaded, so he had the opportunity to fuck around in life and chase his fucking dreams. The rest of the world is not so lucky. Some of them have to be at work at eight in the morning stacking shelves. He had nothing to lose. Right, come on, let's get on with this farce.'

I exit the car and light a cigarette, and glance back through the window. Geordie turns to the back seats and gives both Flaky and Robbo a hefty thump to their thighs.

'Oi, dim and dimmer, we're here. Wake up!' he bellows.

Flaky lets out a shrill scream, whereas Robbo merely grunts.

'Are we here already? That was easy,' he says, wiping sleep from his eyes as he exits the car.

'No, it wasn't easy. It was a nightmare,' I begin. 'You try sitting up front with someone who thinks he can drive like Lewis Hamilton but has the ability of Mr Bean.'

'You had the chance to sit in the back, but insisted on being upfront,' Flaky retorts as he bends over and touches his toes.

'Too right! I wanted to be as close to the steering wheel and handbrake as possible. Did you ever actually pass your driving test, Geordie?' I quiz. I've never actually seen his licence.

'Of course I did,' he replies a little too quickly for my liking as he slams the driver's door shut.

Robbo sparks up a spliff and stares at the motorhome.

'I guess our van hasn't arrived yet,' he comments, as he sucks on his joint. Flaky drops into a downward dog yoga pose.

'Maybe we're all going to bunk down together. Those things can sleep five. Four bunk beds at the back and another bed above the driving area.'

I don't correct them. I'll derive much more enjoyment by witnessing their gormless expressions when Hammer explains the sleeping arrangements. It has become increasingly apparent the trio of fearless survivalists are going to be in for an exceptionally large and uncomfortable shock. A shock they somehow overlooked whilst sat in a warm, air-conditioned office in London, surrounded with canapes, Icelandic spring water, and aloe-vera infused wet wipes whilst being ego massaged by executive producer Jerry Bloomberg.

I open the boot of the car and retrieve four large backpacks and hand them out.

'Will, I'm still not happy about this,' Flaky states.

'About what? The fact we agreed to be on Celebrity—I Will Survive? The fact we have to spend two nights in the highlands of Scotland on a survival weekend with Eric the Hammer Harrington, the biggest egotist since Mussolini?'

'No! The fact we're smuggling contraband in our sleeping bags. The contract we signed specifically states not to bring anything to aid or assist us on this survival weekend, apart from one backpack and a sleeping bag.'

'Oh, shut up, your great big tart!' Geordie yells. 'It's one thing, that's all.' Geordie turns to me and smiles. 'For what it's worth, Bill, I think it's fair enough. As you said, let's do this by the rules. Let's play a straight bat with one caveat; we all bring along one item, which will provide sustenance.'

'Thanks for those kind words, big fella. I appreciate them.'

'And what if Hammer searches the sleeping bags?' Flaky persists.

I throw the backpack over my shoulder, slam the boot shut, and lock the car.

'He will search us. He'll search the backpacks. But it's hardly likely he's going to pull out the sleeping bags, unroll them and inspect them... is it?'

'I'd say it could be a distinct possibility,' Flaky replies.

I toke on my cigarette, feel the tension ease, and emit the smoke into the pristine highland air.

'So what if Hammer finds our contraband? Boo-hoo. What's the worst he can do? Confiscate it? Cancel the survival training? Get us booted off the show? It's not the end of the world.'

'Chill, man, chill. It's like sparrow o'clock,' Robbo moans. 'I can't be doing with negative vibes this early in the morning. In fact, I can't be doing with mornings, full stop. Can everyone get a bit of zen?'

We zip up our thermal, windproof, waterproof, idiot-proof jackets and amble towards the motorhome, bickering as normal. As we approach, the door to the van is swung violently open. And there he stands, in front of us, the man himself—Hammer. He's wearing running shoes, tight, full-length jogging pants, and nothing on top. His overdeveloped pecs and biceps are streaked with bulging, pale blue veins which look like they could rupture at any moment. He's clean shaven with short-cropped hair, services style. He rubs a towel over his face then across his glistening chest and abdomen.

'Perfect timing. I've just returned from my fifteen kilometre early morning run,' he pants.

He tosses the towel behind him into the motorhome in theatrical fashion and jumps from the doorway onto the ground, landing in a crouched position with arms and hands in a karate stance. He leaps in the air and does a roundhouse kick at an imaginary foe before issuing a flurry of blows into thin air. To finish he lets out a high-pitched squeal and balances on his left leg, with his right leg cocked at an ungainly angle. He looks like he's trying to get rid of a rather troublesome fart.

'I'm a black dan in four martial arts; karate, jujitsu, sudoku, and hapkido. My name, as I'm sure you're all aware, is Eric the Hammer Harrington, but you can call me, Hammer!'

I glance at Geordie, as he gawps admiringly at his hero.

'And you must be the rock band, the Shooting Tasers. Can't say I've ever heard any of your music. I only listen to the classics; Mozart, Liberace, Beethoven, Brahms, and Barry Manilow. It helps me unwind. Some nights I'm like a coiled spring.'

I exchange a furtive glance with Robbo and Flaky.

'Right, remove all possessions and place everything on the bench. You can keep your wristwatches on but turn your mobile phones off—we're going dark, off grid, covert, undercover. No outside communication with anyone.'

We empty our possessions onto the bench in silence.

'My PA has produced a synopsis on each of you, and I've also got the psychological assessments performed by Dr Kraepelin.'

He pulls a bunch of rolled-up pages from his pocket and flicks through them.

'Excuse me,' Flaky begins, 'but I thought the psychological assessments were confidential and only allowed to be seen by Jerry Bloomberg to determine if we were suitable for the TV programme?'

'Correct. Your point, being?' Hammer murmurs, distracted by his reading material.

'My point is, how did you get your hands on them?'

Hammer half-closes his eyes and smiles.

'That's for me to know and you to find out. I'm the master of stealth. Where there's a will, there's a way. Rome wasn't built in a day. The only rule is—win at all costs. Do you understand?' he snaps.

Fuck me rigid! The guy is a fruit loop. He makes the rest of us look like sane, rational human beings.

'No, not really,' Flaky replies before he is rudely cut off.

'Enough of the parlay! Time is precious! Carp diem and tempura fugit!' Hammer shouts as his attention returns to the psychological profiles.

'This guy is three sandwiches short of a picnic,' Robbo whispers.

By the time we've finished placing our possessions onto the table, Hammer is ready to identify us one by one.

'I can read like a closed book. It's all in the eyes...' he trails off as he stares intently at Flaky, who shuffles nervously. 'Hmm... volatile, short of temper, suffers from a persecution complex. I'd say you're Geordie?'

Before Flaky can answer, he turns to Robbo.

'Passive aggressive, a hectoring pedant and a self-righteous, lecturing hen... you must be, Flaky!'

He fixes his attention on me.

'Indolent, feckless, complete lack of motivation and a predilection for drugs—I'd say you are Robbo. And last, but not least, the big fellow, Will.'

He circumvents Geordie twice, eyeing him up and down.

'Obviously, the leader of the pack. Controlling, secretive, deep, intense. Prefers his own company. Doesn't suffer fools gladly. A paper-thin veneer of patience. A womaniser, a philatelist, and a dog lover. For obvious reasons, you demand loyalty and obedience. I suspect I'm correct in my assumptions?'

I take a step forward. 'Partly. I'm not sure about the womanising and stamp collecting and you...'

'Enough!' he shouts.

He bends down and picks up a large, blue backpack, and slams it down hard onto the picnic table. He unzips it and spills the contents out in front of us.

'This is your kit, the Hammer Outdoor Survival Equipment Pack, in partnership with Icarus Industries, makers of quality camping equipment since 1973. It normally retails for £149.99, but for you, it's free. As you can see, you each have a mess tin, a stainless-steel cup, one spoon, the Hammer fixed blade ultimate pro knife with sheath and fire steel and...'

Geordie's eyes light up as he reaches out and picks up a long black scabbard and yanks on the handle protruding from it.

'Ooh, a machete,' he exclaims excitedly as he swings it violently to his left, missing the tip of Flaky's nose by mere inches.

'You bloody idiot!' Flaky yelps. 'You nearly took my nose off!'

'Oh, shut up, you big, Jesse! You shouldn't have such a big beak, should you?'

Hammer places his hand on Geordie's arm.

'Take it easy, Will. These aren't toys, they're tools. You must treat them with respect.'

'Sorry, Hammer. And by the way, I'm Geordie,' he says almost apologetically.

'Are you sure?' Hammer questions, confused.

'Yeah, I think so.'

I can't believe this conversation is even taking place.

'This is Will or Billy Boy, that's Robbo and old big nose over there is Flaky,' he says, jabbing the machete at each of us.

'Put that bloody machete down!' Flaky yells.

'Slight correction, it's a parang, not a machete,' Hammer explains.

'What's the difference?' Robbo asks.

'Ahem, never mind about that for the moment,' he says, turning his attention back to the survival pack. 'Where was I? Ah yes, a parang, and lastly one bottle each of Hammer's Morning Fluid.'

Whichever bright spark came up with that name needs to take a long, hard look in the mirror.

'Hammer, I've got to say what an honour it is to meet you at last. I've been a massive fan of yours since your first series hit the TV screens a decade ago,' Geordie fawns.

Hammer obviously likes praise and directs his attention towards his super fan.

'Actually Geordie, it's eleven years. Five TV series, six books, one--hundred and fifty-seven guest TV appearances, too many newspaper articles to mention, and fifteen DVDs with bloopers and uncut material. Not to mention my array of online merchandise available directly from my website, Hammer — Leader of the Pack. But I digress.'

'How did you get the nickname, Hammer?' Robbo asks as he spits a rogue strand of tobacco from the corner of his mouth.

Hammer looks wistfully into the distance.

'Good question, Robbo, and one I get asked many times, and it's a bit of a long story.'

Oh, fuck me, here we go.

'When I was in the SAS, on active duty, behind enemy lines, I was known as The Lone Wolf—leader of the pack, but...'

Robbo, much to my delight, interjects. 'That doesn't make sense. How can you be a lone wolf and a leader of the pack?'

Hammer appears a tad annoyed, as he places the tip of the machete under Robbo's chin.

'There are many things in this world that don't make sense, my chubby little friend.'

He pulls the blade away and spins it around in dramatic Ninja fashion.

'As I was saying, when I was with the SAS in Desert Storm, covertly deployed in Iran...'

'Iraq,' Flaky corrects.

'Slip of the tongue. Ahem... we were a team, a unit, a band of brothers. I was the leader of that pack. During one bloody and deadly firefight, I became separated from my comrades. I was chased across deserts, forests, swamps...'

'Forests and swamps?' Robbo says, looking baffled.

'Yes, forests and swamps, infested with crocodiles and piranha fish.'

'I thought piranha fish were native to South America?' Flaky says.

Hammer moves so close to Flaky I think he may kiss him.

'They were a sub-breed which swiftly adapted to desert conditions.'

I throw a sideways glance at Geordie, who is mesmerised by Hammer's complete bullshit. I expected better of him. But hey, when you're in love, you can forgive anything... right?

'May I continue?' Hammer asks.

Flaky looks suitably chastised and nods.

'As I was saying, I was chased across desert, forests, swamps, up mountains, and along narrow valleys with flooded rivers...'

'Are you sure you were in the Middle East?' Robbo questions.

Hammer blanks him. 'I had to live off my wits, my guile, my cunning...'

'You went hungry, then?' I say.

Hammer seems to have gone deaf and ignores me. He is now in some imaginary reverie where he is an amalgamation of John Wayne, Clint Eastwood, Brad Pitt, Tom Cruise, and Miss Piggy.

'I lived in a water drain for over two weeks. But my real battle wasn't with the Iraqis. Oh, no, no, no! Do you want to know who my real battle was with?'

Not really, but I suspect he's going to tell us, anyway.

'The real battle was with...'

He pauses for maximum effect, even though there's not a camera or sound crew within a hundred miles.

'The real battle was against myself—Hammer Harrington.'

'That must have been galling,' I add.

Geordie lets out an audible gasp. What a wanker! And the fairy-tale continues.

'Sometimes, I wanted to surrender and sleep in a warm bed and put a hot meal inside my belly. But I have an iron will, an indefatigable resolve—never surrender! I lived off scorpions, spiders, and rattlesnakes. I drank the blood of a camel mixed with my own urine.'

'Wow! A bit like a smoothie. What happened in the end?' a certain Scottish oaf asks.

'I ambushed a passing motorcyclist.'

'Very handy,' I say. 'In the middle of the desert, swamp, forest, surrounded by piranha fish, crocodiles, and there goes a guy on a Yamaha 500.'

Hammer gives me the glare I've had so many times over the years, usually from teachers, police officers, security guards, and people who open gates for you. It's a stare of utter contempt mixed with suspicion and hatred. It's the—oh, a fucking smartarse—look.

He continues. 'I crashed through three checkpoints, taking out twelve Iraqi guards before finally making it over the border into Qatar.'

'You mean Kuwait?' Flaky corrects, again.

'Yes, I meant Kuwait.' He quickly does a rapid set of squats for no apparent reason. 'Right, I can't stand around here all day talking about my tales of heroism and survival. My mission is to teach you lot how to survive!'

'Hang on,' Robbo begins, 'you haven't explained how you got the nickname, Hammer?'

I'm thinking it was his publicist who coined the name.

Hammer cocks his head slightly. 'Ask yourself this; what does a hammer do?'

He scans us slowly, with raised eyebrows, suspicious eyes.

'Bangs in nails?' Robbo suggests.

'If it's a claw hammer, it could take out nails,' I add.

Hammer is not amused. 'It beats things, it breaks things,' he growls, becoming agitated.

I've got to say, as far as analogies go, that was fucking woeful. A soft feminine voice calls from inside the motorhome.

'Hammer, your breakfast is ready.'

An extremely attractive woman, probably in her mid-twenties, emerges in the doorway and hands Hammer a bacon and egg roll. He grabs the sandwich and takes a huge bite out of it, giving no thanks to his cook.

'Boys,' he mumbles as bits of debris fly from his mouth, 'let me introduce you to my personal secretary, Suzie.'

'Hello, Suzie,' we reply excitedly, admiring her snug fitting activewear.

'Hi,' she replies bashfully before retreating from view.

Hammer continues decimating the bacon roll, but still insists on speaking. Watching someone masticate so early in the morning is not a pleasant experience.

'Okay boys, a few rules,' Hammer says as he idly peruses our personal possessions on the bench. 'Pay attention, because I'm not in the habit of repeating myself, so pay attention. Mother Nature can be your enemy, or she can be your friend. All animals have an innate survival gene. As humans, we are no different. Unfortunately, because of the namby-pamby, left-wing, mollycoddling do-gooders, most of the human race have lost their survival gene. It's been suffocated by the modern world. Nice houses, comfy beds, gas fires, supermarkets, and blue cheese.'

He becomes distracted as he picks a walnut off the table and eyes us all shiftily before inspecting a snap-lock bag full of Robbo's weed. He tuts and shakes his head in an exasperated fashion.

'Hmm, I see...' he mumbles. 'Right, where was I?' he suddenly barks.

'Blue cheese,' Robbo says.

Hammer sidles up to Robbo and holds his palm out in front of him.

'See this,' he says, nodding towards his hand. Robbo's eyes swivel downwards. 'I could kill you with one blow,' he growls.

'That would be totally uncool, man,' Robbo replies nonchalantly.

Hammer takes a step back.

'Ah, a comedian, eh? Do you think funny one-liners and jokes are going to help you survive in the wild?'

'Never really thought about it,' Robbo responds, sporting a stupid grin.

'Ahem, Hammer, you were talking about the rules,' I prompt, becoming increasingly bored with the farce.

He spins around to face me. 'Rules? Rules? The first rule is there are no rules, apart from one rule—survival! Now get your survival kits and stash them in your backpacks.'

We dutifully obey as Hammer watches over us. Robbo picks up his bag of weed and swings it in front of Hammer.

'You don't mind if I take this with me, do you?'

'Yes, I do mind,' he shouts, as he yanks the bag from Robbo's grip and stuffs the last of the egg and bacon roll into his mouth.

'Why?'

'Because you're on a survival course,' he shouts, sending a morsel of egg flying through the air, which fortunately lands on Flaky's forehead. 'If you were shipwrecked at sea or your plane crashed in the Andes, it would be extremely unlikely you'd have your stash of weed on you.'

'You don't know Robbo very well,' I mumble.

'But we're hardly likely to have a backpack, survival kit and sleeping bag on us, are we?' Flaky argues.

A wild look flashes across Hammer's face, as he marches up to Flaky.

'I once killed a man who looked exactly like you. I strangled the life out of him with my bare hands,' he whispers menacingly.

This little nugget of information excites a certain person.

'Wow! Where was that? In Iraq?' Geordie asks excitedly.

'No. It was outside a fish and chip shop in Cleethorpes. A very grim day, indeed.'

'It's always grim in Cleethorpes,' I comment.

'Hammer, when is our motorhome arriving or are we bunking in with you tonight?' Robbo asks with all the innocence only an over-qualified simpleton can possess.

'It will be cramped with six of us in there,' Flaky adds.

Hammer doesn't miss a beat. He places one arm around Flaky and the other around Robbo and chuckles.

'Old friends,' he starts. 'As much as I would love to cosy up with you guys tonight, and sit around the campfire, chew the cud, spin yarns, and talk about battles won and battles lost, I'm afraid it's not possible. Your motorhome is out there,' he replies as he nods in the general direction of the wilderness.

Robbo and Flaky both turn and peer at sand dunes, moorland, and the distant mountains.

Robbo squints. 'Where? I can't see it.'

'Nor me,' Flaky agrees.

Hammer chortles. 'The wild, untouched landscape *is* your motorhome for the next two nights. I only wish it were my mine,' he adds with false melancholy.

'I'm willing to swap with you,' I say. 'If you'd like to sleep rough with the boys, be my guest. If you're short on space in the campervan, me and Suzie could always top and tail.'

Hammer stares at me with malice. 'Ah, another comedian. This is a survival course, not a Mother's Union tea party. You boys will sleep beneath the stars,' he adds.

I glance heavenwards at the dense cloud.

'Stars? More like drizzle. What a miserable shithole,' I murmur.

My only consolation is the abject horror etched on the faces of the fuckwit twins. I've lost count of the number of times I've warned them about this foolhardy adventure. Did they listen? Did they hell! Maybe they'll be listening now, although, the contracts have been signed, and it's all too late... unless one of us dies. Ah, well, never give up hope.

'Right, if you'd like to make your way down to the little hollow behind the sand dunes, I'll be with you in fifteen minutes. It will give you some time to assess your locale. Before you go, I have a question for you? What is the number-one rule of survival?'

His eyes swivel across our faces, as though attempting to read our minds. Good luck with that.

'You said there were no rules?' Robbo states correctly.

'Think again, my slightly overweight friend. Of course, there are rules. Always have been and always will be. Now, what's the number-one rule!' he screams, startling us all.

'Erm, sh... shelter?' Robbo stammers.

Hammer shakes his head.

'Shelter is important, but it is not *the* most important rule,' he replies sagely, arms behind his back, pacing.

'Ooh, I know,' Flaky says, sticking his hand in the air as though he's at primary school. 'Water! You can survive days without food, but only a day or so without water.'

Hammer shakes his head again.

'Water is important, probably the second most vital thing for survival, but not *the* most important.'

He now stares at me and Geordie.

'Hmm,' Geordie murmurs. 'What about your mental state? You know, never give up and all that?'

Hammer looks disappointed in Geordie as he fixes his attention on me.

'Satellite phone and a number for the nearest pizza takeaway?' I say, hoping to raise a laugh.

Hammer purses his lips. Not so much as a titter. The guy obviously has no sense of humour. Suzie appears behind him and hands him a steaming brew of fresh coffee. It smells good. I'd give anything for a cigarette and a hot cup of caffeine right now.

'Thanks, Suzie. I'll be with you in a minute. No!' he shouts, making us all jump. 'The most important rule is assessing your situation. Taking in the lie of the land, the conditions, the weather, figuring which way is north. Five, ten minutes is all it takes. Then you plan. If you fail to plan... you plan to fail, and fail is not a word in my vocabulary.'

Obviously it is, considering he's used the word thrice in his last sentence.

'Excuse me, Hammer,' Flaky interjects. 'Where are the toilets?'

'Hmm, I see. Three comedians in the group.'

He saunters up to Geordie. 'Are you a comedian as well?'

Geordie appears a little nervous. 'Erm, no, not me. I'm deadly serious.'

'Good man. I like the cut of your jib. Right, get your backpacks on and get going.'

'What about all our possessions?' I ask.

Hammer stares at the assortment of wallets, keys, phones, and other detritus on the bench. He picks up the walnut again and examines it in detail.

'Don't worry about them. I'll stash them in the van. They'll be safe.'

He turns and disappears into the motorhome, shutting and locking the door behind him. We stare at each other for a second, then grab our backpacks, sling them over our shoulders and head off down the hill.

'What do you think? Geordie asks excitedly. 'The guy's a legend, right?'

'Wrong! The guy's a first-class twonk and a fruit loop, to boot. A legend in his own underpants. And he's banging his secretary,' I reply.

Geordie halts, mortally offended.

'Don't say that! Hammer's a married man. He's a man of honour and distinction. He'd never cheat on his wife.'

'I agree with you, Geordie,' Flaky chirps in. 'The girl is half his age. Because a woman is young and attractive, and they happen to be sharing a campervan together for a few nights doesn't mean...' He stops mid-sentence as he realises the redundancy of his words.

Robbo smiles mischievously. 'Lucky bastard,' he drawls.

Geordie narrows his eyes for a moment, as though deep in thought. 'Aye, well, even heroes can have flaws. It's not a crime.'

Chapter Fifteen

If I Had A Hammer – Will's Nightmare

We follow a narrow path down to the hollow, which offers shelter from a stiff breeze blowing in off the ocean. We drop our backpacks onto the grass.

'Let's put Hammer's number-one rule to the test, shall we?' I state as I slowly scan our surroundings.

'What do you mean?' Robbo asks.

I shake my head wearily at him. He'd never been the sharpest knife in the drawer, an attribute I put down to his excessive dope intake, but since his car crash a while back, his memory has definitely taken a turn for the worse.

'Assess our situation and make a plan,' I explain with as much strained patience as I can muster. 'I suggest we spend five or ten minutes having a bit of a scout around.'

I turn and head up a steep sandy bank, studded with marram grass. At the top, I gaze down at the long crescent-shaped cove. I can make out a high tide mark where the sea has left flotsam and jetsam behind. A kilometre from the beach are various islands jutting up from the water. I assume this is good, as they will act like a wave break and protect the cove from the angrier outbursts of the Atlantic. I spin around and nearly fall over Geordie, who, for reasons best known to himself, is standing directly behind me. To his rear are Robbo and Flaky.

'What are you doing?' I yell at them.

'Assessing our situation,' Geordie replies, apparently confused at my question.

'No! Not together! I meant split up, fan out. There's no point in us all covering the same ground, is there?' They all shrug. 'Flaky, you head south. Geordie, you head east and Robbo, you head north.'

They all amble away.

'Which way's north?' Robbo shouts as he slips and slides down the dune.

I extend my arm out. 'You see those large rock type things in the distance, between the ground and the sky?'

Robbo follows the trajectory of my arm. 'Yeah,' he mumbles.

'They're called mountains. We are in the highlands.'

'I didn't ask for a geography lesson. I asked which way was north,' he grumbles.

'Jesus man!' Geordie exclaims. 'The highlands are in the north.'

I make my way on to the beach as the bitching slowly fades from earshot. There are craggy outcrops to the north and south of the cove. There's plenty of washed-up driftwood and I've already spotted tangled knots of fishing line, old plastic water bottles, some badly frayed netting, seaweed, and a whole heap of empty mussel and limpet shells.

'Hmm, interesting,' I mutter to myself.

Something far more exciting piques my curiosity. I saunter along the beach for about a hundred metres. A dilapidated wooden rowing boat is half covered with sand. I place my hand on it and rock it from side to side. It moves a little. It would be impossible to move by one man alone. But three men and a giant, and it may be doable.

I slump onto the bleached timbers and rest my eyes. Despite the idyllic setting, I feel nothing but gloom. Two days in the highlands of Scotland, I can just about handle. Four weeks on a desert island in the South Pacific, in sweltering conditions, is a different proposition. I've still not come to terms with it. I'm in denial. Reluctantly, I went along with the idea at the start because I was convinced of two things: I didn't expect us all to pass the psychological profiling, and if we did, then one of us was sure to fail the medical examination. How in hell's name did Robbo pass the medical test, and Geordie the psychological profiling? It beggars belief. Now it's all too late. I can't see any way out of it. Everyone thinks it's going to be a jolly jape, good fun, setting up camp in a jungle. A few games to compete in. It's not! We're going to be tired, hungry, and bloody hot. Sleep is going to be fitful. Tempers will fray; cravings will haunt us day and night as we are removed from our addictions. There's not one positive I can see. It's a disaster in the making. I reach in my pocket for my cigarettes, then realise they're back on the picnic table outside Hammer's motorhome. It only adds to my gloom.

We're standing on an open expanse of moorland as Hammer teaches us our first survival skill.

'You see the little trails through the grass?' he says, pointing ahead.

We all nod.

'They're rabbit runs. That's where you place your snares. Never place them outside burrows. Rabbits are nervous and suspicious creatures. They'll smell your scent if you place a snare outside their burrow and they'll find another way out. What you need to do is to place the snares in the middle of their runs.'

He bends down and sets up a series of sticks pushed deep into the sandy loam, then hooks up a bit of cord around the sticks and demonstrates how the rabbit is snared. He sticks his fist through a loop.

'Imagine this is the rabbit's head. It goes through and when its body tries to follow, the noose tightens. Make sure your sticks are firmly in the ground.'

'I'm sorry, but as you will be aware, from your research, I'm pescatarian and I won't be eating the flesh of any animal,' Flaky snorts in a derisive, holier-than-thou manner.

Hammer laughs as he rests his hand on Flaky's shoulder.

'I can assure you, Flaky, after a few days without food you will eat absolutely anything.'

'No, I won't. There's plenty of vegetation to live off without resorting to barbarism.'

'Shoots and leaves are good for nutrients, and sometimes medicines, but in a survival situation you need protein and fats, and you can only get that in sufficient quantities from meat.'

'I beg to differ,' Flaky sniffs. 'I'll say it again. I will not be eating the flesh of any animal.'

Hammer removes his hand from Flaky's shoulder and takes a deep breath.

'If you don't eat meat, then after a few days, your energy levels will drop. You'll be a burden not only to yourself but also your teammates, your fellow survivalists. Remember, you cannot afford one weak link in a chain, otherwise the chain will snap when put under pressure.'

Flaky doesn't respond, but I can tell by his demeanour he will not budge on the matter.

'I set four snares before dusk last night, so let's see if we've caught anything,' Hammer continues.

'Aye, let's investigate. I've got to say, Hammer, this is all riveting stuff,' Geordie enthuses as he follows closely behind his hero.

We mooch along in silence as Hammer inspects the first three empty snares.

'Ah, look, you see here, the stick has been pulled from the ground. I can't have pushed it in deep enough. It must have been a big buck to have had the strength to do that. He would have been a bloody good meal.'

We wander on for another few metres before Hammer holds his hand up.

'Movement over there,' he whispers.

A few feet ahead is a rabbit trying desperately to escape a snare. Like lightning, Hammer pounces on it and holds it up in the air by the back legs as it wriggles and twists.

'Just because we eat meat doesn't mean we shouldn't respect the animal. It needs to be dispatched humanely and quickly.'

'You're not actually going...' before Flaky can finish, Hammer tightens his grip on the back legs and grabs the neck of the rabbit in the other hand.

'A quick jerk down,' he says.

There's a rather unpleasant cracking sound as the rabbit ceases wriggling. He holds the limp body out in front of him and gives it a smart karate chop to the neck.

'Just to make sure.'

There's a loud thump behind us. We turn around to see Flaky spread-eagled on the ground.

'Oh-oh! Looks like we've got a fainter in our midst,' Hammer says with a chuckle.

Passing Geordie the rabbit, he pulls a bottle of water from his backpack. He strides over to Flaky, kneels down next to him and pours a drizzle of water over Flaky's head while slapping him gently on the cheek. Flaky groans and sits upright.

'That was brutal,' he says, in an obvious fog.

Hammer stands up and grins.

'Survival is brutal, no two ways about it.'

He grabs the rabbit from Geordie and pulls a large knife from its sheath which dangles from his trouser belt.

'Now I'll show you how to gut and skin it.

'Wait, wait!' Flaky cries. 'I can't watch this. I'm heading back to camp.'

He groggily stands up and weaves his way back towards the hollow.

'Oh dear,' Hammer whispers, 'I'm afraid you might have some baggage there.'

'No shit,' Geordie mumbles in agreement.

Hammer flashes his famous alabaster grin and swiftly splits the rabbit down the middle. He pulls out guts and organs and discards them. Next, off come the head and paws, accompanied by the sickening sound of cracking bone. In one swift move, he peels the rabbit's skin off and throws it on the grass.

'Of course, if you were in a survival situation where you were staying put and awaiting rescue, you'd keep the pelt. Turn it inside out and let it dry for a few days and this could make a hand or feet covering. I'll show you how to cook the rabbit.'

He has a quick look around and spots a couple of large sticks, which seem a little too convenient for my mind, considering there's not a tree in sight.

'It needs to be cooked evenly, which means spit roasting.'

He shoves one of the small sticks right up the rabbit's arse and out through its neck. The larger stick is snapped into four smaller pieces as he quickly creates two 'A' frames lashed together by a mysterious piece of cord he had on hand.

'Make sure you roast it well. Better to be overcooked than under. If you get a case of Montezuma's revenge, then you're in a world of pain. Let me tell you.'

'Can we take the rabbit?' Robbo asks, a reasonable request in my opinion.

Hammer flashes his pearly whites.

'No, of course not. If you were really out in the wild, do you think a kindly benefactor would appear out of nowhere and hand you a skinned rabbit?'

'It's possible,' Robbo grumbles.

'This will go into my cooking pot tonight. A nice rabbit and leek stew washed down with a fine bottle of chilled Chablis.'

I hope the bastard chokes on it.

We spend the next four hours getting a crash course in survival from Hammer. He teaches us how to pick our camp site, how to make an 'A' frame sleeping chamber from old driftwood and ferns. How to tie knots quickly and efficiently. We learn what edible shoots and leaves we can eat and what to stay away from. He shows us the dark art of starting a fire with a fire steel then quickly douses it out. He explains how to dig for water and capture rain that pours from rocks. There's a lot of information to take in, and we are all feeling weary. We've been on the go for over twelve hours and the only food we've eaten was breakfast at 4 am. Our bottles of Hammer's Morning Fluid are nearly empty.

'Okay, boys,' Hammer begins with too much good cheer for my liking. 'You've got approximately five hours daylight left to build your shelters and find food and water. I'll check up on you before dusk, see how you're travelling.'

He turns to walk back up the hill towards his motorhome but stops momentarily and scans the horizon.

'I'd get a move on if I were you. You see those dark clouds in the distance,' he gesticulates towards the mountains in the north, 'they're heading this way. It won't be a downpour, I don't think, but it could be persistent drizzle.'

As dark foreboding clouds gather overhead, Hammer heads back to the warmth and security of his luxury campervan... and Suzie.

We amble back to our campground, if you can call it that, slump onto the damp grass and lay out. I detect a certain lack of enthusiasm from everyone.

'I'm starving,' Geordie moans.

'I'm gagging for a cigarette,' I groan.

'What I'd give for a hot vindaloo and a six-pack of lager, followed by a monster spliff,' dreams Robbo.

'I can feel a migraine coming on,' Flaky whines.

I fall into a deep sleep and it's only the cold damp wet brushing my face that eventually makes me stir. I sit up and shoot a glance to my left. The three stooges are all fast asleep. I check my watch.

'Shit the bed!' I exclaim, jumping to my feet. It's six o'clock. 'Wake up, lads! We've got about three hours to go before nightfall and we have no food, no shelter and we're nearly out of water.'

The others moan and groan as they sit up, yawning and rubbing at their eyes.

'Must be all this fresh air,' Robbo says as he scratches at his balls.

'We need a plan and quickly.'

My mind races as I think back to my stroll along the beach a lifetime ago. They all look at me bleary-eyed.

'Right, bugger the 'A' frame shelters, we haven't got time for that nonsense at the moment. There's a boat wreck on the beach. I reckon the four of us should be able to carry it back here. We can prop it up with some driftwood, make a mattress out of ferns and it will keep us dry and warm for the night.'

I don't get the positive response I was hoping for, and it takes a mountain of coaxing and threats to get them moving.

After an hour's strenuous effort, we have the upturned boat in our little hollow. We quickly assemble a thick bed of ferns and throw our backpacks under cover as the mizzle gets heavier.

'Okay, we have shelter,' I announce. 'Now we need to turn our attention to food, water, and fire. Has anyone noticed any streams or gulley's anywhere?'

'There was a little stream I spotted this morning, but I'm not sure if the water is drinkable,' Flaky replies. 'Remember what Hammer said about water, you never know what might have died upstream.'

'We have our mess kits so we can boil the water. Get all our empty water bottles and throw them into your backpack, Flaky. I noticed a load of old plastic bottles on the beach. Grab some from there, rinse them out with seawater, then head to the gulley and fill them up. Geordie, there are plenty of sticks and fishing line on the beach. Grab some and head back to the moorland and set up some rabbit snares. If we don't catch a rabbit tonight, we may get one for tomorrow. Can you manage that?'

'Aye, Billy Boy. I'm on my way right now.'

'Good man. Robbo, you collect firewood. Your best bet is driftwood on the beach. We'll also need some really dry grass or something that's flammable.'

'All right. What are you going to do?'

'I'm going to untangle some fishing line, hopefully with a few hooks still attached to it, and try to catch some fish for our supper.'

I take an hour to untangle the fishing line, find four rusty hooks and fashion something that might be capable of catching a fish. I make my way back to the moorland to collect the guts and organs of the rabbit to use as bait. Back at the hollow, Robbo has gathered a good pile of wood, and Flaky has returned with a backpack full of bottled water. We are working together as a team and it's all coming together, albeit slowly. Unfortunately, the weather has turned against us. The drizzle is getting heavier, and the wind is picking up. I'm dry underneath my waterproofs, but I'm feeling cold, damp, hungry. I also have a raging thirst. If all else fails, we still have somewhere dry to sleep and thanks to our illicit contraband, we'd at least be able to put something into our bellies. I convene an impromptu meeting.

'Listen up, boys. The weather's turning to shit, and we only have about another hour of daylight left. We have shelter, but we need a fire to boil the water and keep warm. As for food, let's hope we've snared a rabbit or caught a fish.'

'I'm not eating rabbit,' Flaky pipes up.

I ignore him and continue. 'We still have our contraband as a last resort. The fact is, I'm on my last legs. We need to eat and drink, otherwise we are going to wake up knackered tomorrow morning! Let's have one last big push and make the most of what daylight we have left. Flaky, I want you to get a fire going. Robbo, check the fishing lines. Geordie, you come with me and see if we've snared a rabbit.'

Rather unexpectedly, there's no bickering and they all nod in agreement. Flaky pulls out the fire steel from his Hammer survival knife and strikes it against the back of the blade. A shower of sparks flies out. It looks promising.

'You need to do it onto the dry stuff first and get a little flame going,' Geordie observes.

Flaky picks up a handful of what used to be dry grass and places it in the middle of the kindling.

'It's damp,' he moans.

I turn to Robbo. 'You really should have put the dry stuff under the boat,' I say, not going too hard on him.

He looks offended. 'You never said that. You said collect driftwood and some dry shit to start it with.'

'Do I have to explain every little detail? A bit of common sense is all you need. Come on, Geordie, let's check the traps.'

We set off towards the moorland.

'Have you noticed that since Robbo's head injury in that car crash, he's got worse? He was a feckless idiot before, but now, well... I don't know. I worry about him,' Geordie says.

'Yes, I've noticed. But let's not mention it, eh? I'm sure he's also aware of it. He was touch and go for a while. All we can do is give him a bit of leeway.'

We drop the subject as we navigate to the open flats and see hundreds of rabbits gently nibbling on grass.

'Wow! Look at that, Billy Boy! I've never seen so many rabbits in one go. Surely, we must have snared one?'

My spirits lift as I imagine myself munching on overcooked rabbit for supper. Twenty-four hours ago, I would have curled my nose up at the notion... but not now.

'We may be in luck. Okay, lead the way, big man, let's check the snares.'

Within a minute, we spot a rabbit struggling in vain to escape the noose set by Geordie. We can hardly contain our glee.

'Well done, Geordie! You did it!'

'Aye. Some of us are natural born hunters. I don't want to blow my own trumpet, but us Scots are at one with nature. I'll let you do the honours, then you can share in the kill.'

'Right,' I say hesitantly.

'Remember the way Hammer did it. Dive on it, free it from the snare, grab it firmly by the back legs with one hand, then a short, sharp tug to break its neck.'

'Yeah, I was there. You don't have to go over the detail. Right, here goes.'

'Be quick! The big bugger is getting feisty. We don't want him to escape.'

'How do you know it's male?'

'Look at the size of him? It would have to be a dominant buck, surely?'

I creep towards the prey and leap on top of it, grabbing its mid-riff firmly with both hands. It emits a startled squawk, which unnerves me. It's obviously terrified.

'Well done, Bill. Now break its neck,' Geordie encourages from a safe distance.

I free the noose from around its torso and grab its back legs firmly. I hold it up in the air as it dances and struggles in vain. It certainly is fat. Its stomach seems to be full of marbles. I suddenly realise it's not a buck but a pregnant doe, not far off from giving birth. Something comes over me and I hesitate. I can't kill it. It's unpleasant enough killing one rabbit. But I'd be killing all the unborn babies—if they're called babies.

'Come on, Bill. Get on with it. The poor animal is petrified. Remember what Hammer said, respect the animal and make it swift. Put it out of its misery.'

I walk over to him with the rabbit still bouncing around in my grip. I thrust it towards him.

'Sorry, I can't. You'll have to do it.'

The look of shock on Geordie's face is intense, but it's swiftly replaced by scorn.

'Ahh! You weak, Sassenach bastard. You English don't have the killer instincts that we Scots do. We've grown up living off the land for millennia. We're at one with nature. It's kill or be killed.'

'Yep, you're right.'

'What?' he says with a startled expression.

'You Scots are natural born killers, hunters. That's why you'll have to do it. My soft English sentimentality prevents me from killing an innocent animal.'

I hand him the rabbit by the back legs. He kneels on the ground and places one hand firmly around its neck. To my shame, I don't have the stomach to watch. I like my meat pre-packaged in plastic from the supermarket.

'I'll head to the campground. See you back there,' I say. 'Oh, bring the guts, organs, and foetuses back with you. We can use them for bait.'

'Foetuses? What are you talking about?'

'It's not a buck, it's a pregnant doe,' I reply as I turn to leave.

'Aye, fuck off, you weak prick. Leave it to me to sort out. Away back to your armchair and slippers, wee man!'

Chapter Sixteen

The One That Got Away – Will's Nightmare

Back at the campground, nothing much has happened. Flaky is still desperately striking at the fire steel, to no avail, and I assume Robbo is on the beach checking for fish.

'It's no good, Will. Everything's wet and I'm getting tired striking this thing over and over.'

'What's wrong with you?' I snap. 'You're a drummer!'

'What the hell has that got to do with anything?' he replies angrily.

'It's all in the wrist. Drummers should have strong wrists! Right, I'm going to see if we've caught any fish.'

I stomp off up the sand dunes, becoming increasingly bitter and frustrated. At the top, I spot Robbo in the distance. I trot over to him. The tide is now a long way out.

'Any luck?' I say, panting.

'Nah, not a sausage,' he replies without a care in the world.

The line is anchored to the beach, courtesy of a large stick stuck in the sand. I pick up the line and follow it towards the sea. After about thirty metres, I spot the four rusty hooks and bait sat forlornly at the edge of the water. I make my way back to Robbo.

'Did you not think to reposition the stick closer to the water's edge? The bait isn't even in the fucking sea! What were you hoping for? A school of passing suicide fish to leap out and impale themselves on the hooks.'

'Don't blame me. It was you who set the bloody thing up.'

'Yes, when the tide was in.'

It's futile. I'm not just fighting Mother Nature but also natural buffoonery. We both walk back to the camp in silence. Flaky is still striking the fire steel without luck. At least the drizzle has abated and there is a pale blue patch overhead, offering a tad more natural light. I look up to see the hulking frame of Geordie heading our way. Without a fire, the rabbit is useless.

'Have you not got that fire going yet? What's wrong with you?' Geordie growls at Flaky as he ambles into the campground.

'Back off! If someone had kept the tinder dry, we wouldn't be in this position!' Flaky retaliates, throwing Robbo an accusing glare.

'Where's the rabbit?' I ask Geordie, who appears distinctly pissed off.

'What?' he snaps back.

'The rabbit, where's the rabbit?'

'It got away,' he mumbles.

'How?'

'It doesnae matter how! It got away, that's all!'

'You couldn't do it, could you? You couldn't kill it?' I chuckle. 'Big tough Scotsman, natural born hunters, it's in your blood. You let it go, didn't you?'

'I did not let it go!' he booms. 'It bit me on the finger. It gave me a start, and I loosened my grip. Before I knew what was happening, it was gone.'

'Yeah, right?'

'Catch any fish?' he asks, quickly changing the subject.

'Nah,' replies Robbo. 'Not as much as a nibble.'

'Pretty hard to do on dry land,' I mutter under my breath. 'Right, I guess it's time to pull out our contraband and divvy it up. At least we'll have something in our bellies,' I state, trying to sound positive.

There's an eerie silence from the others as they glance sheepishly at each other.

'Come on, grab your backpacks and let's see what each of us has brought.'

They reluctantly make their way to the boat and pull their backpacks out. I'm puzzled by their demeanour, and I have an impending sense of doom.

'You go first, Flaky,' I encourage.

He puts his hand into his backpack, pulls out the sleeping bag and unrolls it. He holds up a book.

I'm stunned. 'A book?'

'Not just any book. It's the Good News!' he says, trying to sound cheery.

'No, it's fucking bad news!'

'It's the Bible,' he says, looking for validation.

I nod my head slowly, trying to resist the urge to butcher him with the parang. I turn to Robbo. His eyeballs swivel back and forth between Geordie and Flaky, an action that doesn't fill me with confidence.

'Robbo,' I prompt.

Robbo unfurls his sleeping bag and retrieves a small snap-lock bag from the hood and holds it aloft.

'A bit of weed, tobacco, and a packet of cigarette papers,' he states almost apologetically.

I rub my hands through my hair and don't even comment. My gaze now falls on Geordie.

'I've got something that will cheer us all up,' he says, beaming like a village idiot.

He holds up a large thermos flask. I'm praying to God it's full of tepid tea or coffee or clean water. Dare I believe?

'What's in it?' I ask in a low whisper.

'The finest single malt whisky. A full litre of it!' he exclaims as though he's just discovered electricity.

I rub at my chin and make my way to a large boulder and slump back against it. I'm beaten... defeated.

'What's wrong with you?' he asks in an incredulous tone. 'I thought you'd be pleased. A wee dram will warm you up and blow your troubles away.'

My repressed anger finally erupts.

'You useless pack of fuckwits!' I yell as I advance towards them. 'I said bring food or water!'

'That's not true,' Robbo mumbles. 'You said bring something of sustenance,' he explains.

'It's true, Will, they were your exact words,' Flaky concurs.

'Give me strength!' I bellow into the darkening sky. 'Give me fucking strength!'

Geordie is already pouring himself a shot of whisky. I rush towards him and grab the cup from his hand and throw it against the boulder.

'You fucking idiot! We haven't eaten for over sixteen hours; we're all dehydrated and you're going to knock back whisky!'

'Whoa! Calm down, Billy Boy! Calm down!'

I suddenly feel drained and empty. I walk over to the pile of sticks, pick up the fire steel, and strike it against the knife. A flurry of sparks erupts, but Flaky is right, everything is too damp.

'I need to take a number two. If you'll excuse me,' Flaky says as he heads off.

'Make sure you cover it up. I don't want to be standing in your shit in the middle of the night,' Geordie calls out after him.

Geordie holds his hand out towards me.

'Here, give me a go,' he says.

I pass him the fire steel as he kneels beside me and strikes away. Robbo wanders over to a rock and prepares to roll a joint. A few minutes pass in silence before Geordie nudges me and nods towards Robbo.

'Look at that moron,' he whispers. 'Watch his face once he's rolled his joint and realises he's got nothing to light it with,' he chuckles.

I stare at Robbo and see the funny side as I let out a dispirited laugh. Geordie stops striking, as we both fix our attention on Robbo. He carefully inserts a roach into the end, licks it up and down the seam, and twists the end of the cigarette paper into a wick.

'Here we go,' Geordie says under his breath.

Sure enough, Robbo fumbles about in his pockets for a lighter. Geordie sniggers. A baffled expression spreads across Robbo's face. His searching becomes ever more frantic. He stops for a moment and closes his eyes, then smiles. He slips his hand inside his jacket, pulls out a lighter and sparks up the spliff.

'I do not fucking believe it!' Geordie exclaims.

'You couldn't make this shit up,' I reply.

I walk over to Robbo, who emits a plume of aromatic smoke, then offers me the joint.

'No thanks, but if you could roll me a plain cigarette, I'd appreciate it.'

'Sure thing, man. No worries.'

'Robbo, can I ask you a question?'

'Yeah, fire away, man.'

'You see that pile of sticks over there?' I say, pointing at the unlit pyre.

'Yeah, what about them?'

'Did you notice Flaky has been trying to set it alight for over two hours?'

He looks offended by my question. 'Hey look, I know all right. I should have kept the kindling dry, but you can't blame me for the weather.'

I nod at him and hold my tongue. 'Yep, sorry. I won't mention it again,' I reply as I pat him on the shoulder. 'Do you mind if I borrow your lighter?'

He reaches into his pocket and passes it to me.

'Thanks. I'll bring it back in a minute.'

'Cool,' he says.

I walk back to Geordie, who shakes his head in disbelief.

'Do you think it's the dope or the car crash?' he enquires.

'Bit of both,' I reply, as I crouch down and flick the lighter.

A few embers sparkle and dance, but still nothing will take a hold.

'We need dry material to generate heat,' I moan.

'Hang on, I have an idea,' Geordie says as he bounces to his feet and heads towards the boat.

⟫⟫⟫ ⟪⟪⟪

By the time Flaky returns from his ablutions, the fire is in full flight.

'Hey! I thought I could smell smoke,' Flaky yells out as he stumbles down a dune. 'How the hell did you get it going?'

'It's called perseverance,' Geordie replies, 'and a bit of technique. You were doing it all wrong,' he chuckles to himself. 'Hey, hang on a minute, Billy Boy, what did you actually bring?'

'Sorry?' I reply as I stare into the flames.

'Contraband! You had a go at all of us for what we brought, but what did you bring?'

It's completely slipped my mind. Rushing to my backpack, I pull out my sleeping bag and dig around inside until I locate my prize and yank it out.

'A tub of raisins!' I declare.

'Ooh, good one, Will. Raisins are super nutritious. Full of natural sugars,' Flaky states with glee at the prospect.

Pulling the lid off the box, I hold it out. Flaky and Geordie grab a handful and stick them in their mouth, as I follow suit. I've never tasted anything as good. Robbo hands me the rollie as I pass him the tub of raisins. I spark it up and inhale and receive a sudden dizzy rush to the head, followed by an intense, relaxed feeling.

'Oh, yes, that's the ticket,' I murmur to myself.

I lean back against the boulder and feel my troubles slip away. Flaky is busy setting up the mess tins and pouring the collected water into them. Geordie holds his thermos flask up in the air and waggles it from side to side.

'Who's up for a wee drop?' he shouts.

'Aye, why not,' I reply.

As I sip on whisky and smoke my cigarette, my thoughts return to my aching belly. The raisins, or maybe the whisky, seem to have revived my spirits and given me a spurt of energy, and the sun has broken through for the first time all day as it slowly begins its descent into the sea. I walk over to the fire and throw my cigarette butt into the flames. I drop my gaze to the ground and stare at the empty cockle and mussel shells.

'How did these shells get here?' I ask absentmindedly.

'Not sure,' Flaky replies. 'I suppose seagulls pick them up and eat them here.'

There's a moment of silence before we suddenly stare at each other.

'Hey, I've an idea,' I declare.

'Me too,' Flaky smiles. 'You first.'

'Cockles and mussels. The tide's out and there's two craggy outcrops at either end of the cove. 'I'll bet my last quid those rocks are covered in shellfish. Go on, what's your idea?'

'Seaweed… the beach is strewn with the stuff. It's the cabbage of the sea. I've eaten it plenty of times and not only is it tasty but also nutritious.'

'Right, grab two backpacks. Geordie, come with us. Robbo, you tend to the fire. We're going to get our supper.'

⇝⇜

An hour later I pull the first mess tin of mussels and cockles from the embers as Flaky retrieves a mess tin of rubbery looking seaweed cooked in water, a drop of whisky and with a handful of raisins thrown in for good measure. I drop a mussel into my mouth and savour the salty meatiness.

'Okay boys, let's tuck in.'

We devour the first batch in double quick time as a second batch is hastily placed over the coals. As our stomachs fill, whisky is dispensed, and joints smoked. We laugh and joke at the day's proceedings. It's funny how quickly things can turn around. I can't say the day has been an overwhelming success, but we survived it and learned a few things along the way, despite our mentor going AWOL.

Eventually, silence descends over the camp as weariness takes over and we each ponder our private thoughts. Hammer didn't make an appearance as promised, obviously more pressing matters to address in his motorhome.

I retreat to the upturned boat, lay out my sleeping bag, discard my waterproofs, but keep my clothes on as I snuggle down. The earthy scent of the heather and ferns offers a comforting feeling. It's not long before Robbo does the same. Flaky appears and grabs his Bible.

'I'm going to read a few passages before I bed down,' he informs me as my eyes close.

'Whatever,' I murmur as sleep descends.

'That's bloody odd!' I hear him exclaim in the distance.

'What's odd?' Geordie asks.

'I'm missing the entire Gospel according to Luke,' he states in an exasperated manner.

'Nothing odd about that. We had to start the bloody fire with something,' Geordie replies.

Chapter Seventeen

Wake Up Little Suzie - Will's Nightmare

The bitterly cold seawater stings my face. Crouching on the shoreline, I scoop another handful and repeat the process. As uncomfortable as the feeling is, it banishes the last vestiges of sleep from my aching body.

It was an awful night's slumber. I wipe my face on my jumper and glance at my watch—6:12 am.

I clamber back to the top of the sand dunes and stare down at the upturned rowing boat which holds my comatose pals. My gaze wanders to the giant mountains in the distance, the ocean to the west and the emerald moorlands dead ahead. The cry of gulls, the gentle warble of land birds and the steady snoring of Geordie and Robbo assault my ears. My eyes finally fall upon Hammer's motorhome in the distance. A figure appears and performs star jumps. I watch the self-proclaimed hero and nutcase for a few moments until he stops his ridiculous callisthenics and jogs off.

'Hmm... it's worth a try.'

My stomach rumbles. I need three things; caffeine, food, and nicotine... and I know where I can get them.

Grabbing a backpack from our sleeping quarters, I make my way up the hill.

My three raps on the motorhome door are met with silence. I try again.

'Who is it?' a soft feminine voice asks in a worried tone.

'It's me, Will Harding.'

'Hang on,' she replies.

A few seconds elapse until the door opens ever so slightly.

'If you're after Hammer, you've missed him by about ten minutes. He's gone on his run, and he'll be a good two hours or more,' she says, unsure, suspicious.

'Yes, I saw him leave. Actually, it's you I wanted to see. I want to ask you a favour.'

She appears even more wary.

'Calm down. I'm only after a cup of coffee and some food.'

The door opens a little more as she brushes her hair back.

'Oh, I see.' She pauses. 'I'm sorry, but if Hammer finds out I'd given you food I'd lose my job.'

I nod at her. 'Okay, fair enough. I should never have asked. Please accept my apologies.'

I turn to leave.

'Wait! I suppose a cup of coffee would be okay. I must admit, I couldn't live without it,' she says, smiling at me.

She opens the door fully and invites me in.

'Instant or plunger?' she enquires.

'Plunger, please! And make it strong.'

As she prepares the coffee, we strike up conversation.

'How did you become PA to Hammer?'

She peers wistfully out of the window. 'Through a friend of a friend. His last PA left to have her first child.'

'What exactly does it entail, being a PA?'

She lets out an ironic laugh as she pours boiling water into the plunger. The smell alone has my pulse racing.

'Initially, it was to manage his website, his social media, and respond to emails, which is something I'm good at.'

'I sense a "but" coming.'

She pours the coffee into two cups.

'Let's sit outside. I get claustrophobic being stuck in this bloody motorhome all day.'

As we make our way outdoors, I grab my cigarettes and lighter from the countertop. We take up seats around a wooden picnic table. I pull a smoke out and spark up.

'Could I have one?' she asks.

'Sure, I didn't realise you smoked.'

'I don't when I'm around Hammer. He forbids it.'

She places the cigarette in her mouth as I hold the lighter up to her. She takes a lusty drag, holds it for a moment, then puffs out the smoke in a long steady stream.

'Oh, that feels good.'

I take a delicious mouthful of coffee and relax.

'It's funny how you miss the little things,' I comment. 'Anyway, you were saying about the job?'

'The first few months, that's what I did; I updated his website, posted to social media once a day, answered his emails. As time went on, I began to cook and clean for him. Eventually, we became lovers.'

I'm surprised by her candour.

'You don't seem happy about it?'

She takes a sip of her coffee.

'He's a man-child and my God, he's a boring old sod. He talks about himself constantly. It's his only topic of conversation. If I talk to him about books or films, or even my own life, he zones out. And he's a terrible lover. Selfish, rough, and quick, if you know what I mean.'

I laugh. 'I'm sure most women would say the same thing about their partners. If you're unhappy, why don't you leave?'

'I intend to. I need to find another job first. He pays well and so he should; it's non-stop with him.'

'Hey, I have an idea. We... I mean, the band, are looking for a virtual assistant to do exactly what you're doing for Hammer. At the moment, our wives do everything, and they've done an excellent job, but things are only getting busier, and we all have young kids. Would you be interested?'

I can tell by her brilliant smile she is.

'Would I ever!'

'Grab a pen and a piece of paper and I'll give you my wife's email address.'

She's back in a shot. I scribble the details down.

'Fire off an email to my wife with your resume attached. Tell her I told you to get in touch.'

'Wow! Okay, I'll do it while Hammer's on his run. You definitely want a virtual assistant, not a personal assistant?'

'Yeah. You can work from anywhere.'

'What's the money like?'

'I wouldn't have a clue. The girls take care of all that. I'm sure they'll pay the going rate... whatever that is. Where do you live, normally?'

'I have an apartment in Leeds.'

'Good. I'm in the Dales, so we're only an hour away.'

I stub my cigarette out and finish the dregs of my coffee.

'I better get back to the lads. Looks like mussels and limpets for breakfast.'

I hand her my cigarettes and lighter.

'You better put these back inside. We don't want Hammer becoming suspicious.'

I pull on my backpack and turn to walk back down the hill.

'Wait!' she cries. 'How would you all like some bacon and egg rolls and a flask of coffee?'

I smile at her. 'Suzie, you're a superstar!'

⤜⤛⤛ ⤜⤛⤛

Back at the campground, the boys are all sitting around the smouldering fire, dispirited and grumpy.

'Where've you been?' Geordie asks, apparently annoyed at my leave of absence.

'To get us breakfast.'

'You're hilarious,' he replies.

'I know... it's why you love me.'

I unzip the backpack and hand out the rolls.

'Bacon and egg sarnies for us three and a veggie burger for Flaky. Oh, plus a two-litre flask of coffee, four packets of dried rice for our evening meal tonight, four litres of bottled water, and a packet of smokes. I think I'm going to enjoy my last day.'

⤜⤛⤛ ⤜⤛⤛

It's five in the morning, and we're all eager to depart. It was a dreadful night as a thunderstorm passed through, bringing a chilly blast with it. We're cold, sore, and hungry.

As we trudge up the hill towards the motorhome, and our escape, I remember something.

'Oh, shit!' I exclaim.

'What's the matter?' Flaky asks.

'The rabbit traps—I meant to get rid of them. I'll have to head back down. I can't bear to think one might get snared and die of hunger or get picked off by a predator without a chance.'

'Don't bother, Bill. I got rid of them yesterday when the pregnant doe got away.'

I laugh and slap him on the shoulder. 'You mean when you let it go?'

'I'm telling you I didn't let it go. Not intentionally.'

'Of course you didn't, big man, of course you didn't.'

As we near the motorhome, Hammer appears in the doorway.

'Aha! Boys, you're all up early. I'm about to go on my run. Anyone care to join me?' he says with a cocky grin.

'No thanks,' Robbo says. 'We'll grab our stuff and be on our way.'

'Fair enough. I hope you enjoyed your survival weekend and I trust you picked up some vital skills.'

'Enjoyment is not the word I'd use,' Geordie moans. 'And what happened to you?'

'I'm not sure what you mean.'

'You were supposed to be training us in the art of survival. You spent a few hours with us on day one and we didn't see you at all yesterday!'

Hammer grins. 'I won't be there for you on your tropical island. Sometimes the best way to learn to swim is to be thrown in at the deep end.'

'Is that right?' Geordie snarls. He's definitely fallen out of love with his ex-hero. 'I'm sure you were paid a pretty penny by the production company for this weekend. As far as I'm concerned, you haven't earned your keep.'

Suzie pushes past Hammer and hands us a carrier bag full of our possessions. We quickly scramble about, retrieving phones, keys, and wallets. Hammer jumps down from the step and walks over to Geordie and slaps his hand on his shoulder.

'Now, now, Geordie, don't be like that. Anyway, I'm paid for what I know, not what I do,' he offers with a smarmy grin.

'One, two, three...' Geordie counts as he glares at the hand on his shoulder.

Hammer throws me a puzzled glance.

'What's he doing?'

'Erm, I'd suggest you remove your hand from his shoulder before he reaches five,' I reply.

'Four...'

Hammer quickly withdraws his hand and takes a step back nervously. He checks his watch.

'Right, I'm off for my run. Suzie, have a bacon and egg roll waiting for me when I get back. There's a good girl.'

He turns and jogs off into the distance.

'Wanker!' Geordie says, scowling.

As we turn our mobile phones on, there's the constant sound of clicks and dings as messages and notifications filter through. I notice a text message from Fiona and open it up.

'Hmm... interesting. Suzie, guess what?'

'What?'

'How does fifty grand a year sound, for starters?'

'You're joking!' she screeches.

'I jest ye not. The job's yours if you want it?'

She does a little dance on the spot. 'Yes, yes, yes! When do you want me to start?'

'ASAP. In fact, why don't you come back with us? We're kipping at Geordie's tonight, but I can drop you in Leeds tomorrow. You can meet Jackie and Fiona. What do you say?'

She puts her hand to her mouth and sports a worried frown. 'I couldn't... could I? You mean leave him, right here and now?'

I smile at her. 'Your life, your choice.'

She rushes into the motorhome. 'Give me five minutes to get my shit together and leave him a note!' she shouts.

I spark up a smoke and amble over to Geordie. 'Take it easy on the drive home. And remember, the first stop is Maccas. That's how ravenous I am.'

'I hear you loud and clear, Billy Boy, loud and clear.'

Chapter Eighteen

Homage To Dinkiad Bay

I drive slowly along the narrow streets of Dinkiad Bay. It's over two years since I last set foot in the place. I'd grown up here as a boy and spent years here after the band had first split up. It holds many fond memories for me. I'd always imagined Nan and Gramp's old house would have become our weekender. A place where Jackie, me and kids could retreat to once a month and kick back. It has a nice sandy beach for the boys to play on, and it's only an hour's drive to the Cairngorms National Park and many fantastic walks and sights. However, Jackie isn't keen on my old village. She finds it insular and cliquey and feels like an outsider. She also doesn't much care for the tiny fishing cottage, having become accustomed to the vast spaces of our Edinburgh townhouse and all the modern conveniences that came along with our renovations.

Jackie suggested we put the cottage on the market, as we still have to pay rates and a handyman to cut the grass and check on the place occasionally. I know it makes sense to sell, but I can't bring myself to do it and I'm not sure why. It could be the memories the place holds for me or maybe deep down it's my fallback. When, and if, my world turns to shit, I'll have somewhere to escape to.

I pull up and gaze at the cottage. It seems to shrink in size with every visit. I check my watch—it's midday. Flecks of rain carried on a blustery breeze dot the windscreen. The sun has retired for the day behind grey leaden clouds. I'm feeling peckish. There's no food in the house apart from dried pasta and maybe a packet of dried soup. A visit to the Fisherman's Way is on the agenda. I can grab a bite to eat and catch up with Margaret and Stereo Stan.

I lock the car and set off on foot. Not a single soul do I see on my five-minute stroll. It's a ghost town. Dinkiad Bay was never a busy place, but it's far quieter than I recall.

In the pub, Stereo Stan is behind the bar polishing glasses. He throws me a lazy glance before doing a double-take.

'Well, I never, I say, well, I never! If it's not my old chum, Geordie! Margaret, we've got a visitor! I say Margaret, we've got a visitor!'

'Stan, you haven't changed a bit,' I lie.

He appears diminished in every aspect. He's smaller and has less hair, which is now more white than grey. He's also lost weight, but not to his benefit. He looks gaunt. Margaret comes bustling out from the kitchen and throws her arms around me, kissing me on the cheek.

'Geordie, good to see you! How long are you staying? Have you brought the wife and kids with you?'

'No, they're back in Edinburgh. I'll be here tonight, possibly tomorrow. I'm here to check on the house, and air it out a bit.'

'Stan, pour Geordie a pint! What are you waiting for!' she scolds her husband.

'Aye, of course. What will it be, Geordie? A pint of bitter?'

I nod. 'You still serving food, Margaret?'

'Yes, and dinner, too. Although we only do lunches in the summer months when it's busier.'

I scan the pub. There's an elderly couple sitting in a corner eating a meal, and that's it.

'Things are tough?'

'You could say that. I'm not sure how long we can keep going. Anyway, you don't want to hear about that. Come and sit down and fill me in with all the news.'

Stan places the pint on the bar.

'First one's on the house, I say, first one's on the house.'

'Cheers, Stan. And I'll have a Guinness pie with chips.'

He nods as I grab my pint as Margaret leads me by the elbow to a table. I spend fifteen minutes relaying my latest information and gossip to her until my meal arrives, at which point she heads back to the kitchen. The food is good, and I devour it in no time. I notice the elderly couple gingerly make their way out of the door. A pang of melancholy washes over me. The whole place, the village, and the pub, has an air of decrepitude. It's like a dinosaur going through its final death throes. Maybe Jackie is right?

I get a fresh pint, then rack up the balls on the pool table. As I chalk the cue, Stan makes his way over to collect the dinner plates and cutlery. I know he'll chew my ear off.

'There are only two trawlers left in the village now, Geordie. I say, only two trawlers left.'

'Is that right?'

'Aye. When you were a lad, there was ten moored up in the harbour, I say, ten. Do you remember?'

'Yes, I do.'

'During the summer, this used to be a bustling seaside town as well. They had donkey rides on the beach, fishing trips, and a helter-skelter. All gone now,' he adds wistfully.

'Yes, I remember. I wasn't allowed on the donkeys once I'd passed the age of eight. They said I was too big.'

I blow chalk dust off the end of my cue, line up the ball, and prepare to break off. As Stan picks up the plates, a knife falls to the floor.

'How's that wife of yours getting on? She's a bobby dazzler, that one. You're punching well above your weight there, Geordie. I say, you're punching well above your weight!' he guffaws.

He bends down to pick up the knife at the same moment I take my shot. I've put far too much power and topspin on the ball, thanks to Stan's ill-timed comment. The cue ball sizzles across the table at the speed of light, hits the jaw of the middle pocket and becomes airborne. It's like a blinding flash of white lightning as it spears through the air until the unstoppable force hits an unmovable object, in the form of Stan's orange shaped noggin. There's a sickening crack.

'Oomph, hell fire!'

It's followed by the crash of crockery as he crumples to the floor like he's taken a headshot from an ace military sniper. I race over to him and pull him to his feet. A golf ball shaped lump magically appears on his temple.

'Sweet mother of Jesus,' he murmurs. 'What the bloody hell was that? I say, what was that?'

'I'm sorry, Stan. It was the cue ball. It clobbered you on the noodle. Margaret!'

'Sweet holy buggery. I feel like I've been kicked in the head by a Clydesdale. Let me sit down, I say, let me sit down.'

I navigate him to a chair as Margaret appears behind the bar.

'Whatever's the matter?' she asks, looking concerned.

'Get him a stiff brandy. I've felled him with the white ball.'

Margaret rushes the brandy to him, and Stan gratefully knocks it back in one go and requests a refill.

'Huh, he can't be that bad if he wants another one,' Margaret grumbles, whose concern for her husband has quickly evaporated.

'How many fingers am I holding up?' I ask him.

'Five, I say five, I say five, I say five.'

Fuck me! I've turned Stereo Stan into Quadrophonic Stan with one reckless shot. I know the inhabitants of Dinkiad Bay can tolerate him repeating things twice, but four times, that's pushing the boundaries.

'Okay, good. Take it easy for the rest of the day. If you start getting headaches, I suggest you visit the quack.'

'What do you mean, *start* getting headaches? It feels like some bugger's parked a pickaxe in my melon.'

'You really ought to be more careful in the future,' I advise. 'You've no spatial awareness.'

Margaret returns with the brandy.

She smiles at me. 'Oh Geordie, how we've missed you. There's never a dull moment when you're around.'

'Speak for yourself, I say, speak for yourself.'

Normal service has been resumed.

⤜⤛⤙ ⤚⤜⤛

Two tiny dots on the horizon bob up and down. I pull a spliff from my pocket, light it, and relax back on the bench. I'm delaying the inevitable. The thought of rumbling through Nan's chest of keepsakes hoping to find some correspondence from my father doesn't fill me full of cheer. I miss her, and Gramps, terribly, and gazing at old photos and trinkets will only heighten my sorrow. If only she could have lived long enough to see me get married and see her great-grandchildren. At least she won't have to witness my divorce. I wonder what advice she'd give me if she were still alive? Forgiveness is what she would have advised. Forgive, make up and try again, and keep on trying until we both get it right.

I'll confront Jackie a day or so after my birthday party, once all the guests have left. I've no idea how she'll react. She's unpredictable at the best of times. I'm not even sure how I'll react. I swing from anger to sadness to loneliness and back again. I take a last drag on my spliff and stamp it out. I now realise the dots in the distance are the two remaining Dinkiad Bay fishing boats returning to shore. I wonder how long before there's only one—then none? Nothing remains the same.

※※※ ☙☙☙

The house smells musty, so I open up the windows to let some fresh sea air blow through. I can't believe how tiny the kitchen and my bedroom are. I can now see the place through Jackie's eyes. It belongs in the past, not the present, and definitely not the future.

I locate the chest from the bottom of Nan's wardrobe, stagger downstairs with it into the living room and place it on the floor. With a full bottle of Glenfiddich twelve-year-old single malt, and a dram glass sitting on the table, I'm ready to begin. I open the chest. There are a bunch of letters parcelled neatly together tied with pink ribbon, but none are from my dad. Love letters between my Gramps and Nan, letters from overseas relatives, postcards, and for some unknown reason, a receipt for eight ounce of loose leaf tea from 1956 for a shilling and thruppence.

The entire experience takes less than an hour, and it wasn't as bad as I'd let my troubled imagination envisage. It was bittersweet as I pored over old photos of myself as a youngster. There's a lovely photo of Nan, when she was probably Jackie's age, early thirties. She was a bit of a looker and had a fierce determination in her eyes. I had a good long chat with her and shed a tear or two. It's ridiculous... talking to a photo. I not only miss Nan but I'm missing my family now. I pull my mobile out and call Jackie.

'Oh, hi love, you got there all right then?' she says breezily. 'I'm just preparing the evening meal.'

I don't know what to say.

'Geordie, hello, are you there?'

'Ahem, yeah, just ringing to let you know I got here safely. How are the boys?'

'They're outside playing in the fort. They've been little buggers all day, fighting and carrying on. They always seem to play up when you're away.'

I grin at the thought of them.

'Anyway, I read them the riot act and told them it's dinner, bath, and bed. No TV for them tonight.'

'Don't be too hard on them. They grow up quickly. Enjoy them while it lasts.'

'Easy for you to say. Did you find any letters from your dad?'

'No. Nothing.'

'Oh, I see,' she says, appearing distracted. 'Listen, I'll have to call you back. Wallace is standing on the top of the fort waving a branch around. If he's not careful, he'll have his brother's eye out.'

'Jackie, before you go, I want to say, whatever happens between us, I'll always love you.'

'Geordie, what is it? What's wrong?'

Now I've worried her. 'Nothing, honest.'

'Are you okay? Are you depressed? If you are, I can jump in the car and be with you in three hours. I can get Mam to come over and look after the boys.'

'No, really, I'm fine.'

'You don't sound fine. You sound upset, sad.'

'I'm sorry. It's looking over these old photos. It's made me a little melancholy, that's all.'

'Are you sure? Wait...'

I hear her footsteps over the tiles, then her voice.

'Wallace Kincaid, put that stick down this instant and if I see you with it again, I'm confiscating your Lego set for an entire month! No, you're not William Wallace. You're a little boy acting silly. Now put it down.

Do I make myself clear? Good! Sorry about that... the little shit. Do you know what he said? He said he was William Wallace, and he was going to free the Scots from English tyranny forever. I wonder where he gets that from?'

I chuckle to myself. 'I best go. I can see you've got your hands full. I'll call you tonight once the boys are in bed.'

'Geordie, are you sure everything's okay?'

'Yes.'

'I mean it, I can be with you in a few hours, just say the word.'

'No, don't talk daft.'

'Are you sure?'

'I'm sure. Right, I'll speak to you later. Love you.'

'I love you too.'

I lean back on the couch and sip on whisky, not thinking about anything in particular. My eyes fall onto the wooden chest. There's nothing remarkable about it. It appears to be made from birch or similar wood. It's simply a plain old chest. And yet, something is not quite right. I take it back upstairs and place it in the wardrobe. As I'm heading back down, my mobile rings.

'Billy Boy, what's happening?' I ask.

'Ringing to see if you're okay?'

'I see. Jackie's rung Fiona, to ask you to ring me to check that I'm not suicidal or anything.'

'No, not at all. Can't a mate ring for a chat?'

'Liar.'

'Okay, Fiona said Jackie was worried about you. You were acting odd. To which my reply was, you are odd, what's odd about that. Anyway, you have previous.'

'You're referring to the hanging. I told you I wasn't trying to hang myself.'

'No, of course not. You were at a loose end. It's perfectly normal for someone to be standing on a chair with a noose around their neck. And there's the time you played Russian roulette with Chas. Often, when I'm feeling bored, I juggle hand grenades with the pins pulled out, it really brightens my day, makes me feel alive.'

'Bill, I'm all right, honestly. I'm going to mow the lawn, pluck a few weeds, have an afternoon kip, then I'll be heading back to the pub for my dinner. After that, a few hours TV followed by bed. I'll probably set off home tomorrow, mid-morning.'

'Okay, I know you're fine. I'm only pulling your pisser. Did you find your dad's letters?'

'No. It was a long shot.'

'Hey, maybe the chest has a secret compartment?'

'It's not Treasure fucking Island. It's a plain box. There are no hidden drawers or secret levers to pull.'

'Listen, I've got to go. I can hear Fiona yelling at the kids. I'll see you in a few days for your birthday bash. Catch ya.'

⤙⤛⤙ ⤚⤚⤚

'Hey up, here comes trouble, I say, here comes trouble,' Stereo Stan yells as I walk into the pub.

He's sporting a large white bandage around his head, as though he's been involved in some military conflict. It's past six and there are a handful of customers dotted around the bar. The smell of fresh fish, oil, and batter loiter in the air as I lick my lips. I shake hands and exchange pleasantries with the locals and some old pals.

After my dinner, I enjoy maybe one too many pints with the old gang before heading home. As I saunter along deserted streets, swathed in amber lamplight, I'm feeling a damn sight better than when I arrived. My melancholy has dissipated. My spirits are in the ascendency.

Perhaps Bill is right? Maybe there is a logical explanation for Jackie's behaviour? I just want to go back to normal. Anyway, even if she has been playing the field—what about it? It doesn't mean she doesn't love me. It doesn't stop us from being together. We will need to work it out, of course, but I'm not the man I used to be. The rush to anger is no longer as strong as it was, thanks to Dr Engle.

As I push open the garden gate, I get a picture in my head of Nan and the damned chest. Something is bugging me about it.

I kick my shoes off, switch on the TV and pour myself a nightcap. I flick around the channels until I settle on a home improvement show. Some guy with a blinding smile is talking as he picks up a tape measure and marks a piece of wood. He's building a fucking rocking horse, as you do when you're an amateur woodworker with nothing but a saw, hammer, and tape measure. They always make it look so easy.

Tape measure... tape measure. I leap from the couch and rush to the cupboard underneath the stairs and grab a tape measure from the toolbox. Scampering up the stairs, I feel a glug of excitement. In Nan's bedroom, I pull the chest out from the wardrobe and measure the height of the box. Twenty-four inches on the outside. Removing the contents, I measure the inside—eighteen inches. My hands tremble as I study the floor of the chest. Nothing appears untoward until, in one corner, I notice a screw sitting proud of the base. I grab it and pull. The floor of the chest lifts. Underneath, another pile of letters stares up at me.

Chapter Nineteen

Birthday Boy

Geordie opens the boot of the Range Rover as I hold open the door of the bakery. The baker and his assistant tentatively tiptoe outside, each holding one side of a board containing the cake.

'Easy, boys,' I encourage.

The cake is huge. A perfect replica of a Gibson bass guitar.

'Hey, Billy Boy?'

'What?' I reply.

'I forgot to bring my wallet,' Geordie says as he pats at his trouser and jacket pockets.

'Really? What a surprise.'

'No, honest, I left it on the kitchen counter... I think. Can you do the honours?'

'Okay, but I want paying back. Tight Scottish git.'

'Charming. It's your best mate's birthday and you won't even shout for the cake. Did you hear that, boys?' he says to the bakers as they carefully place the cake in the car.

'He is from Yorkshire,' the baker says with a smile.

'How much do I owe you?' I ask as I retrieve my wallet and pull two fifties from it.

'That will be £260, thank you.'

'How fucking much! £260 for a bit of sponge cake and icing!'

The baker looks disapprovingly at me.

'Tut, tut, tut,' Geordie says. 'This isn't simply a cake. It's a work of art. These two guys are no different from us. They're artists, they just work in a different field.'

'I'm in the wrong profession. I don't think anyone has ever paid me £260 for one of my songs, and they take a damn sight longer to put together than a bloody cake.'

'True. But these guys can only sell a cake once, whereas you can sell a song a million times.'

I reluctantly hand over six fifty-pound notes and leave my hand outstretched, waiting for my change. The baker gleefully stuffs the money into his apron and produces a set of sparklers, which have been fashioned into 'Happy 40th'.

'And it's another £40 for the candles,' he adds.

'Hmm... how incredibly convenient. Make sure you declare the VAT in your tax return. The black-market economy hurts everyone. Think of the National Health Service,' I call out to them as they disappear into the bakery.

Geordie slams the boot shut and we both climb into the car. 'Nice looking cake,' Geordie comments.

'Yep, very nice, considering it didn't cost you a penny.'

'You'll get your money.'

We set off on the short journey back to Geordie's pad.

'How are you feeling... you know, with the Jackie situation?'

'Not good.'

'Any chance you can elaborate?'

He pulls up at a red light and turns to me. 'If it wasn't for what I think she's been up to, then this would have been the happiest day of my life. Ever since I had those therapy sessions with Dr Engle, things have changed. I've been able to control my rush to anger. My thinking is clearer. When I went back to Dinkiad Bay and found Dad's letters, it was like a weight was lifted from me. All my life I thought he'd abandoned me, but he hadn't. When Iain was born, money was tight. Dad joined the merchant navy and made good money that he'd send back to my Mam. But being away at sea for extended periods is not good for any marriage. He came home from one trip and found out Mam had shacked up with another bloke. They got divorced. This other bloke got my Mam hooked on drugs and the rest is history.'

'Why did your Nan never show you the letters or let your dad have access to you?'

'I'll never know. I assume she thought it was for the best, you know, like when someone is adopted—make a complete break from the past.'

'How did you feel when you found his death certificate?'

'It was a rollercoaster ride. I'd spent an hour reading his letters and felt on top of the world. Then I had a silly notion; I'd try to track him down and we'd reconcile. He could come and live with me, Jackie, and the boys. Then I came across his death certificate. It knocked the wind out of my sails. I suppose the only positive is it was over twenty years ago. If it had been recent, I'd have always felt guilty I hadn't tried to find him sooner.'

'What did he die of?'

'A ruptured congenital aortic aneurism.'

'In layman's terms, Dr Kildare, if you don't mind.'

'It's a bulging of the artery wall near the heart. Congenital means he had it since birth.'

'Similar to my dad... how bizarre. How old was he?'

'Forty.'

'Shit! Same age as you. I hope it's not an omen.'

'You're such a cheerful soul, aren't you?'

Two loud beeps from behind indicate the traffic lights have changed to green. Geordie sticks his head out of the window.

'If you blast your horn again, I'll rearrange your face—free of charge—wanker!'

'I can see the therapy sessions helped.'

The car lurches forward. 'Where were we?'

'Your dad, the letters, the death certificate.'

'Aye, that's right. So, even though it wasn't good news, it drew a line under everything for me. Even going back to Dinkiad Bay made me realise the past has gone and there's no point in mourning over it. I have a new life now with Jackie and the boys. Except...'

'Except you're still not sure if she's cheating on you?'

'Aye. If it wasn't for that, I'd be living the dream. It's like I'm cursed. Why can't I have what other people have? I want happiness. Is that too much to ask for?'

'I don't have any answers for you, Geordie. Apart from this, you don't know the truth. Not yet. What are you going to do?'

'My options are limited. I can stick my head in the sand and turn a blind eye...'

'You will have a blind eye if you stick your head in the sand.'

'Can you be serious for a minute? This is my marriage we're talking about,' he responds angrily.

'Sorry,' I wince.

'If I turn a blind eye, then we stay together. If I confront her about it and it's true, my world collapses.'

'You've left out one other possibility.'

'What's that?'

'You confront her about it, and she has a perfectly plausible explanation.'

'I think you're clutching at straws, Billy Boy.'

'I'm not clutching at straws. She's not my wife.'

'You know, your bedside manner leaves a lot to be desired.'

'So, what's your plan?'

'I'm going to confront her. Day after tomorrow, once all the guests have left.'

'And say what?'

'I'm going to tell her about me bumping into Carly at the same time she was allegedly having lunch with her. Then I'll tell her about us following her to the house.'

'Whoa! Slow down, big fella! Don't bring me into this. She doesn't need to know both of us followed her. That's only going to cause problems in my marriage. If you're going down, then at least be man enough to go down alone.'

'Thanks for your support.'

'In fact, don't even mention we followed her. Say you were driving past when you saw her go into some stranger's house.'

'No. I've had enough of the lies and deceit. It leaves a nasty taste in my mouth.'

We round a corner and pull up outside Geordie's house.

'Eh up, looks like Robbo and Flaky's mob have arrived,' I say, pointing at the cars parked opposite the house. 'How many guests have you got coming to this birthday shindig?'

'About forty.'

'You don't have forty mates! In fact, you've only got two; me and Robbo—three if you include Flaky.'

'Listen, pal, I know plenty of people. I'm a man about town. A social butterfly. I deliberately restricted the list as I wanted it to only include people I have a connection with, you know, a bond. If Jackie had her way, we'd have two hundred people arriving.'

We carefully transfer the cake from the car to the marquee in the back garden and place it on the centre table. Robbo and Flaky sidle up to us.

'Nice one,' Geordie,' Robbo drawls. 'You've hired caterers. Clever idea.'

'I cannae take the credit. Jackie said she didn't want to do any cooking or clearing away. These guys do everything. The marquee, the tables, and chairs, plates, cutlery, and they come the next day to clear it all away. Mind you, it's cost me a small fortune.'

'You always complain about the price of things,' Flaky chips in.

'Aye well, your wife doesn't throw money around like confetti,' he replies, as he storms off.

'What's wrong with him?' Robbo says.

'Stressed,' I reply.

Flaky and Robbo are oblivious to Geordie's marital shenanigans. I glance around the garden at the throng of children running wild.

'What time does the party kick off?' Robbo asks.

'In about an hour. Come on, let's go inside and see if we can help with anything.'

After putting streamers up, fixing the children some food, then vacuuming their mess up, I need a beer. Geordie's outside on the patio stood on a chair. I saunter out and stare up at him.

'What's the problem?'

'One of the kids has pulled the wire out of the back of the speaker.'

'I'm ready for a beer. What about you?'

'Nah, I'll hang off.'

'Shit the bed! I think I'm hearing things. I've never known you refuse a beer.'

He stops tinkering with the speaker and looks down at me.

'The thing is, ever since all this began, I've cut down on the booze. I've hardly touched a drop in the last few weeks. I'm scared if I have too much to drink, it will loosen my tongue. I need to be in control of my faculties when I ask the *big* question.'

'But it's your birthday, Geordie. You're entitled to a few drinks.'

'No, honest. I'm fine. You help yourself. They're in the spare fridge in the pantry.'

As I walk back inside, I pass Fiona, and we exchange a kiss.

'How's it going, big boy?' she asks.

'Yeah, good. And you?'

'I'm really looking forward to it. I can't wait to let my hair down. It's been a while. I love a good party.'

I smile at her. 'Yeah, I know what you mean.' I turn to leave, then stop. 'Fiona, Jackie hasn't said...' I stop myself.

She pulls a frown. 'Jackie hasn't said what?'

'Nothing.'

She's even more puzzled. Never stoke a fire unless you want more heat.

'It can't be nothing. What were you going to say?'

'Jackie hasn't said how much all this cost, you know, the caterers?'

'I think she said it was about £1200 for the food and marquee. But then you've got to consider the bar and how much everyone drinks tonight. That will be on top. Why?'

'I thought for our next party we could hire caterers. Makes things easy, don't you think?'

She eyes me suspiciously. 'Yeah, I suppose it does.'

I give her another kiss and head into the pantry. As I open the fridge and procrastinate over which brand of beer to crack open, the creak of the pantry door behind me makes me spin around.

'Oh, hi Jackie. Just grabbing a cleansing ale.'

She purposefully closes the door and leans against it. 'I'm glad I've caught you in here,' she begins in a hushed tone. 'I've been trying to get you alone for some time.'

What the hell does that mean?

Chapter Twenty

Birthday Surprise

My head goes into a spin as a dozen salacious thoughts jostle for position in my feverish mind. I smile nervously, the sort of false smile that makes your cheeks hurt.

'And why's that?' I reply, grabbing a beer and hastily cracking the top.

'Have you noticed anything strange about Geordie lately?'

'Lately? I've noticed something strange about him for the last twenty--odd years,' I laugh as my heart rate subsides.

'I'm being serious, Will!' she snaps.

'Sorry. In what way do you mean?'

'He's been aloof, stand-offish, and withdrawn for the last month or so.'

'He's been through a lot lately. The therapy, finding his dad's letters and his death certificate. These things can affect a person.'

She frowns. 'It's not that. Those things were kind of therapeutic for him. It was like he'd found closure. There's something else going on. You're his best friend. Has he said anything to you?'

'No, apart from his usual gibberish.'

She doesn't look convinced. 'There's something else...'

'What?'

She gazes at the floor. 'It's a delicate matter,' she says as her cheeks flush red. 'He's always had, erm, an active...' she stops again.

'An active?' I prompt.

She coughs. 'Erm... an active libido... sex drive. And the thing is... well, we haven't had sex for over a month.'

This is embarrassing. 'I see.'

It's the best I've got. I'm a rock star, not a bloody marriage guidance counsellor!

'The thing is... I think he's having an affair,' she adds.

Slap my arse with a kipper!

'No, not Geordie. You and the kids are his life, his world. He'd never do that to you.'

Her face brightens a little. 'Are you sure? You're not lying to me, are you? I know you two are as thick as thieves. Please Will, if you know something, tell me the truth. I'm not going to erupt and spoil the party. It will hurt, but we can get over it. We can get counselling, but I need to know the truth.'

She's almost in tears. I place my hand on her shoulder.

'I swear, Jackie. If Geordie was playing the field, then I'd know. Give him a bit of time to come to terms with what's happened recently.'

A tear drips down her cheek. I pull a tissue from my pocket and hand it to her. She dabs her face, then blows her nose noisily into the tissue and hands it back to me... not that I wanted it.

'Okay. Thanks. I'm overthinking things. I'm sure it will turn out all right.'

She opens the door and slips away.

I'm standing in the kitchen with Robbo and Geordie, talking about our next album we've yet to record. The caterers are busy outside putting the finishing touches to the marquee and the outside bar. Every time someone opens the door, savoury aromas of spit roasted meat wafts through the air.

'Hmm... that meat smells good,' Robbo comments. 'What is it?'

'Lamb and beef roasts,' Geordie says. 'They've also done a nut roast and have some salmon fillets for Flaky and Gillian. That's the problem these days you've got to cater for everyone; vegans, vegetarians, lactose intolerant, dairy intolerant, peanut intolerant... it's a fucking nightmare. What happened to the good old days when you served it up and people either ate it or they didn't?' he moans.

I glance at Robbo, who shoots a worried look back.

The sliding door to the patio is rudely flung open as the head of catering storms in, obviously annoyed.

'Excuse me, Geordie, but can I have a word?' she demands.

'Aye, what's the problem?'

'I don't want to seem ungrateful, but one of your friends outside insists on helping, and to be quite frank, he's more of a hindrance than a help.'

'Is it a skinny bloke with a big nose, glasses and bears an uncanny resemblance to a giant rat?' Geordie asks.

The woman nods, embarrassed. 'Ahem, well, yes. In the right light, he does have a passing resemblance to a rodent. He's questioning the ingredients of the nut roast and changing the seating arrangements. If you could have a quiet, discreet word, I would appreciate it.'

'Aye, that's Flaky. Leave it to me. Discretion is my middle name.'

He marches towards the back doors and sticks his head outside.

'Oi, Flaky! You ferret-faced-fucker! Get your arse in here now!'

The party has been underway for over three hours. The food is fantastic, and everyone is in the back garden having a wonderful time... apart from Geordie. He's still wound up like a grandfather clock. Music is gently emanating from the outdoor speakers; the kids are busily playing on the fort and I'm standing with Robbo and Geordie opposite the marquee, next to the bar which is set up in the middle of the garden. The music abruptly stops, followed by the "tink tink" of a wine glass.

'Excuse me, ladies and gentlemen,' Jackie's voice booms out through the speakers.

The laughter and chatter fade away as all eyes turn to the marquee and the large table that holds the birthday cake. She holds up a raft of papers, stares at them for a few seconds, then discards them.

'Ahem, I had a speech prepared. All nicely written down... but bugger it. I'm going to improvise.'

There's a throng of people in front of us and I can only see Jackie's head.

'Where's the birthday boy?' she shouts.

Geordie lifts his arm, reluctantly, as everyone turns to stare at him amid a clatter of handclaps and whoops.

'Okay, so where do I begin?' she says.

'At the beginning!' Robbo hollers as he sparks up a spliff. Jackie smiles benevolently at him.

'No, I won't start at the beginning. I'll start at the end... or near the end,' Jackie replies.

'What the hell does that mean? Geordie hisses.

'It doesn't mean anything,' I say. 'Chill, brother.'

Jackie continues. 'You all know Geordie very well. You're his friends. So, you'll be well aware that living with him is not the easiest task in the world.'

There're a few chuckles from the gathering. I glance at the big fella. He has his eyes closed.

'The fact is, I have a confession to make,' she continues.

Her words are met with a chorus of good spirited oohs and aahs.

'Confession is good for the soul!' Flaky yells, laughing like a drain.

I glance over at Fiona and hold my hands out. She shrugs her shoulders. Whatever Jackie is about to say, my wife does not know what it is.

'The fact is,' Jackie continues to an enthralled audience, '... the fact is... I've been cheating on my husband.'

Chapter Twenty-one

Birthday Ruse

I feel heady, as though I'm about to pass out as a few nervous laughs ring out around the garden but the overriding mood amongst the party guests is confusion and embarrassment. Geordie sways slightly. I spin around to the barman behind me.

'A whisky,' I whisper. 'No, make it a double, no, a treble.'

He frantically screws the top off the bottle of whisky and pours a treble. I go to hand it to Geordie, then stop and slug it down myself.

'Sorry, same again!' I command.

Before he repeats the procedure, I grab the bottle of whisky from him and fill a wineglass to the brim with the amber fluid. I pass it to Geordie.

'Here, old pal, take a sip on this,' I say, hoping it will calm him.

He grabs the offering and pours it down his throat in one hit.

Robbo leans over to me. 'What the fuck is going on?' he murmurs.

'Not good,' I reply, as my words dry up. There's no stopping Jackie's words, though.

'Would you all like to know who I've been cheating on my husband with?' she calls out with a big smile on her face.

It's followed by silence as her captured audience shuffle nervously. She's certainly not picking up on the feedback. At the back of the marquee a curtain is pulled aside as a smallish, pudgy man strides forward with arms splayed forth, as though he's won an Oscar.

'Is that him? Is that the guy we saw at the house?' Geordie stammers.

I squint. 'Yeah, I think it is.'

'Why is she humiliating me like this? Have I been such a bad husband and father?'

'Hello everyone! My name is Rupert Vermeer, and yes, it's true, Jackie has been secretly visiting me once a week for a few months now,' he declares without an ounce of shame. 'I am a painter!' he declares, like it should impress everyone.

'What did he say?' Robbo whispers.

'He said he's a painter,' Flaky replies.

'I'll get his number afterwards. Our downstairs bog could do with a lick of paint,' he says as he draws on his joint.

'Not that sort of painter, you clown! He's a famous oil painter,' Flaky explains.

Jackie takes the limelight once more.

'Without further ado... Rupert, will you do the honours?'

'Of course, my dear.'

He heads towards the curtain he emerged from and pulls it down. There's a chorus of gasps.

'Geordie, open your eyes!' I urge.

He slowly, flutteringly, opens his eyes.

'Geordie, birthday boy!' Jackie calls out. 'Would you like to come forward to cut your cake and say a few words?'

He staggers towards the marquee as I follow closely by his side. He bypasses the table which holds the cake and falls to his knees in front of the giant oil painting. Front and centre is the image of Geordie, dressed in a kilt and tartan tunic. His hands clasp the hilt of a Claymore, speared into the ground. He's proud, defiant, indefatigable. To his right is Jackie, also dressed in ancient highland garb. Her arm encircles his. She sports a crown of heather. Her eyes burn fire. To Geordie's left are his sons, Wallace, and Robert, dressed in kilts, both holding a targe in their hands. The background is of moorland and heather, in the distance, the mountains of the highlands. A wild stag studies the figures from afar. It's perfect, the symbolism exquisite. The big fella rocks back and forth, then sniffs. I can honestly say I've never seen Geordie shed a tear before.

❯❯❯ ❮❮❮

I tuck the girls up in bed, give them all a peck on the forehead, tell them I love them and slip quietly out of the bedroom. I bump into Jackie as she emerges from Wallace and Robert's room.

'The party's going well,' I say.

'Yes, it is. Now we've got the kids to bed, we can really let our hair down.'

We walk down the stairs together.

'Jackie?'

'Yes?'

'You know earlier, in the pantry, our chat about Geordie?'

'What about it?' she says, throwing me a worried look.

'The thing is, he's been aloof and distant because he thought *you* were the one having an affair.'

She stops and turns to me. Her worried look evaporates. It's replaced by a deadpan stare.

'Now, where would he get such an idea?' she says, fixing me with a steely glare.

'Erm, I'm not sure.'

'Och aye the noo,' she says.

Her words nearly knock me off my feet.

'Sorry?'

'You heard,' she replies as she continues heading down the stairs, leaving me stranded. 'Hedgehog quills and auctions in Budapest. You two must think I'm stupid. By the way, if you ever follow me again, I'll cut your balls off. I'll be issuing the same warning to my husband first thing tomorrow morning.'

I can't believe it! We've both been stitched up like a pair of kippers!

Chapter Twenty-two

Down In The Ghetto

I'm sitting in the back garden relaxing, catching a few rays as I nibble on a plate of green olives and sip on an ice-cold glass of pinot grigio. The walled garden is looking magnificent. Vines creep along the old bricks and brush up against the cherry and plum trees. Bees work tirelessly as they hover around foxgloves, petunias, and lavender. The sweet scent they emit is delicious. I rest my eyes and let all thoughts recede.

It doesn't last long.

I hear the clank of the gate handle and glance down the garden path. I'm surprised to see Scotty. I'd just about given up on him as I haven't seen him for over a week, not since the day before my birthday bash. I study him as he trudges towards me. There's something wrong. His demeanour is downcast, as he sticks his hands deep into his pockets and stares at his feet. I thought he was making progress. Each time he'd previously turned up to do his chores, he appeared a little brighter, a tad more confident. All that is gone.

'Take a seat,' I say. He drags a chair out from under the table and slumps into it. 'I thought you'd thrown the towel in. I was contemplating cutting the grass myself this afternoon.'

'Sorry, Geordie.'

'No apology required.' I smile but get no response. 'Do you want a drink? Lemonade, ginger beer, Tizer? I can't offer you coke as Jackie won't allow it in the house. The caffeine, you see. She doesn't want the boys drinking it.'

He half lifts his head. 'Where are they?'

'The boys? Jackie's taken them off to get new school shoes. They shouldn't be long. Although, once my wife gets a taste for shopping, she can be gone for hours. She has a PhD in spending money. I don't know how she does it.'

I receive a weak grin. 'What's happening? Are those lads bullying you again?'

He shakes his head.

'Well, something's amiss.'

'It's my dad. He's dead.'

⋙ ⋘

I place the cheese and tomato sandwich on the table in front of him and hand him a cool glass of lemon cordial. He takes a good slurp before attacking the sandwich like he hasn't eaten in days. He wolfs it down in less than a minute. The sustenance revives him a little.

'I assume you want to talk about it, otherwise you wouldn't be here. What happened?'

'He worked at a retail park out of town. Drove a forklift. A shelf collapsed as he was lifting some slate tiles onto it. He was crushed to death.'

Christ! What a way to go!

There's silence as he shuffles a few crumbs around his plate.

'When did it happen?'

'Seven days ago.'

'How's your ma coping?'

'Not good. He was a bastard, but she still loved him. I'm worried about her... you know, her state of mind. She sits in her chair rocking back and forth, mithering about how we're going to cope financially.'

'I'm sure there will be compensation from the company. They pay insurance for such eventualities.'

'It's not that simple. He wasn't on the books; it was cash in hand. That way, he could still sign on the dole and get his other benefits.'

I lean back in my chair and sigh. 'And how are you doing?'

He shrugs. 'I know this sounds wrong, but I feel relieved. I'm actually glad he's dead. He made my and ma's life a misery. We're better off without him. But...' He trails off.

'But, what?'

'I feel guilty for feeling that way.'

'Don't. Only you and your mother know what it was like to live with him. You're feeling guilty because society expects people to grieve over the passing of a close relative. Be true to your own feelings and damn the rest of the world. Having said that, you also need to be tactful, and use some guile.'

'Whaddya mean?'

'You know, don't go around telling everyone you're glad he's dead—especially not your mother. You'll gain nothing by it, and people will think you're heartless, cold.'

'We're home!' Jackie's voice calls out.

Wallace and Robert come rushing down the steps into the garden.

'Scotty, do you wanna kick the footy?' Wallace yells as he grabs the football and boots it into the air.

'Not now, Wallace,' I say. 'Now's not the time.'

'Oh! But why not?'

Scotty glances at me. 'It's okay. I don't mind. It will stop me thinking about things.'

He jumps to his feet. 'Okay, I'll go in goal. We'll play penalties. Five shots each. Whoever loses has to go in goal after me.'

'Yeah!' Robert cries. 'I'll be Rangers.'

'No, you can't be Rangers, I'm Rangers,' Wallace protests.

'No! You can be Kilmarnock.'

'I don't want to be bloody Kilmarnock!'

'Wallace... language,' I scold.

I pick up the plate and glass and head into the house. Jackie is busy unpacking.

'I see the waif and stray has returned. I thought we'd seen the last of him,' she comments coldly.

Her callous words would normally provoke an admonishment from me. But not this time.

'It's his dad. He was killed in a forklift accident.'

She drops the shopping and clasps at her mouth.

'Oh, my lord! When did it happen?'

'A week back. That's why we haven't seen the lad. From what he says, it sounds like his mother is in a bad way—mentally. I think we need to offer our help.'

'Yes, of course, but I'm not sure what we can do apart from convey our sympathy.'

'The family is going to need more than sympathy. I don't think the lad's eaten for days the way he scoffed the sandwich down I made him. I think we should drive him home and meet his mother. Get the lay of the land.'

A thoughtful expression crosses her face as she taps the back of her wedding ring on the countertop.

'What's the matter?'

'I'm upset for the wee lad, and his mother, but...'

'Go on.'

'I don't know how to say this, but I think you're getting too close to the boy. He's not our responsibility. He'll have relatives and there are always the authorities. He's not our concern. We have our own bairns to think about.'

I glare at her as she returns to unpacking the shopping.

'You amaze me. You're quite willing to have a dozen or more direct debits flow out of our bank account each month to various charities around the world but when it comes to actually getting your hands dirty, in your own backyard, you say it's not our concern.'

She averts my eyes. 'I'm simply saying...'

'I know what you're saying. You're eager to help people you'll never meet so you can pat yourself on the back and tell yourself that you're a good person. Lessen the guilt you feel for living in luxury.'

'That's unfair!' she snaps.

'Is it? Well, you can do what the hell you like, but I'm going to help the lad out whether you like it or not.'

She storms from the room and slams the door behind her, making the glasses in the cabinet rattle. I pick up the knife and carve two more thick slices of bread.

⤞⤝

The car weaves through the city until we enter one of the outer suburbs that wears a bad reputation. Long gone are the elegant Georgian and Victorian townhouses or the flashy new high-rise apartments, housing the wealthy and upwardly mobile. They are swiftly replaced by rundown stone tenements with bricked up windows, doors embossed with steel facades, dangling drainpipes, and amateurish graffiti staining the walls. The place smells of desolation, abandonment, and hopelessness.

I glance at Jackie, who is mute in the passenger seat. Her left hand rests against her forehead as if to shield her eyes from the sights.

'This place is like a war zone. We shouldn't have brought the boys. I said it was a bad idea,' she murmurs.

My eyes wander to the rearview mirror. Wallace and Robert were their usual chirpy and boisterous selves a few minutes ago, but now they stare out at the grim landscape in silence. They've led sheltered lives.

'If you take the next left and drive to the very end, we're the last house on our road,' Scotty says.

'Aye. No problem.'

The next street is a good deal better than the wasteland we've driven through. 1940s style semi-detached council houses adorn the road. Most appear well kept and tidy, if ultimately drab. I pull the car up outside the last house and stare, appalled at what I see. A small front garden is strewn with debris; an old bath, a broken sink, plastic pipes, a rusted motorbike frame and numerous other detritus. Weeds and long grass entrap the objects in a labyrinth of greenery. The living room window has a piece of cardboard in the bottom right-hand corner covering a hole in the glass. The front gate is hanging off its hinges. There are tiles missing from the roof, and dreary, dirty curtains hang haphazardly from broken rails.

'Thanks for the lift, Geordie,' Scotty says reluctantly as he alights from the car.

'My pleasure. Hey, hang on. I'll pop in to offer my condolences to your ma if that's all right.'

Jackie throws me a sideways glance of panic. Scotty is reticent at my suggestion.

'Aye, I suppose,' he mumbles.

I jump from the car and turn to Jackie.

'I won't be a jiffy.'

'Can we come in?' Wallace asks.

'No.' Jackie swiftly rebukes him.

Scotty doesn't even attempt to open the garden gate and hops over it instead. I try to push it back, but it's wedged. I give it a boot and it falls off its hinges.

'Shite!'

'Don't worry about it. It's been knackered for years,' Scotty says as he pushes at the front door with his shoulder.

I follow him into the hallway. Things don't improve. There's a small grubby mat lying forlornly on bare floorboards. A damp, mouldy smell pervades the atmosphere, mingling neatly with the peeling paint on the walls.

'Ma, ma!' Scotty calls out. 'It's only me. I have someone with me.'

'I'm in here, son,' a timid female voice replies.

'What's your mother's name?' I ask quietly.

'Isla,' he says as he turns left into a room. 'Ma, I'd like you to meet Geordie.'

I enter the living room, which is in keeping with my first impressions. The woman looks up at me, confused.

'Pleased to meet you, Isla. I'd like to offer my condolences and pay my respects during this most difficult time. If there's anything I can do to help, no matter how big or small, then all you need to do is say the word.'

She offers me a weak smile. 'Thank you, Geordie. Scotty has told me so much about you. I'm so grateful you found some work for him. It's much appreciated. Teenage boys are a worry.'

She rises awkwardly to her feet. Behind her haggard and creased features was once a woman of beauty. Dead eyes rest beneath long, limp hair. She's thin... way too thin.

'I'm being rude. Now, you will stay for a cup of tea, won't you?'

I'm torn between wanting to flee this house of horrors or doing the right thing.

'I'd love to stay for a cuppa, Isla, if it's not too much of an imposition. But you sit yourself down and I'll make it.' I turn to leave.

'I'll give you a hand,' Scotty pipes up.

'No. You stay with your ma. I'm quite capable of hunting down the teabags and a few cups.'

As shocking as the hallway and living room are, the kitchen takes it to a new level. Dirty crockery is piled to overflowing in a tiny sink. The linoleum on the floor is ripped and stained. A tap constantly drips as a breeze wafts through another broken pane, making a grey net curtain perform a mournful ballet. I fill the kettle with water, then inspect the cupboards.

'Sweet merciful shite,' I murmur to myself. 'Old Mother Hubbard is alive and well.'

Opening the fridge, I retrieve a carton of milk and sniff it. It's still fresh. A creaky floorboard makes me swing around. Jackie is standing in the doorway with her hand over her mouth in apparent disbelief.

'Oh my, oh my. I've never... I mean... I didn't know people could live like this.'

'Unfortunately, it's all too common. Why don't you chat with Isla, you know—woman to woman and see if there's anything we can help her with.'

'Yes, of course.'

As I line up four cups on the counter, Scotty appears and slouches in the doorway, staring dolefully at the floor.

'Penny for your thoughts?' I ask as the kettle hisses its annoyance.

'You shouldnae have come in,' he mumbles.

'And why's that?'

'I didn't have much dignity to begin with, but now I have none.'

The boiling water froths around the tea bag as I ponder his words.

'You're embarrassed?' I question as the last cup is filled.

'Aye. Embarrassed, ashamed, humiliated. It's bad enough living here without people you care about having to see it.'

I reach out to him and place my hand on his shoulder.

'Believe me, this is a palace compared to some digs I lived in when the band split up the first time around.'

'You're just saying that,' he mumbles sullenly.

'I shit you not. I lived in one house that didnae have a roof. It was nice and airy, if a little chilly on a night.'

He tries to stifle a smile.

'And another place I was squatting in had no power, gas, or running water. I used to have to take a shovel, dig a hole, and shit in the back garden.'

'How did you end up like that?'

'When the band split up, I hit the bottle, upped the drugs, and blew all my money. For two years I lived like a hobo on the streets in and out of squats, sleeping rough.'

'How did you turn it around?'

'My Nan found me passed out in a Glasgow alley one Christmas Eve. She took me back home to Dinkiad Bay and sorted me out.'

'Then what?'

I pour milk into the cups and give them a quick stir.

'She got me back on my feet and away from drugs. After a few years, Billy Boy turned up at my local pub searching for me. The rest is history. If it hadn't been for Nan and Bill, God only knows what would have happened to me. Sometimes it's okay to accept help from those who care about you. At some point in your life, when you've found your feet, you'll come across someone who needs your help. That's when you pay it forward. What goes around comes around. Does your ma take sugar?'

'Wouldn't matter if she did, we don't have any.'

Chapter Twenty-three

Helping Hand

Scotty has found a couple of old, battered Action Men which Wallace and Robert are happily playing with in the back garden, which is also overgrown and out of control. I watch them for a moment from the window. Jackie is having a good old natter with Isla as Scotty and I attempt to clean the kitchen and stack the crockery away. As we finish, Wallace and Robert rush in.

'Scotty, Scotty! Come outside. Me and Robert have built a cave for the Action Men to live in!' Wallace screams.

Scotty throws me a slightly bored look but responds with enthusiasm towards the children.

'Really? Okay, I'll come. But guess what?'

'What?' my boys say in unison.

'We need to find food and water to survive in the wilderness.'

All three rush out of the back door as Jackie enters the kitchen bearing a sombre, troubled expression. She folds her arms and taps her right foot aggressively on the floor.

I choose my words carefully. 'Jackie, I know what I'm about to say won't sit easily with you, but I'll say it anyway. We... or at least *I*, need to help them out. There's no point arguing about it because my mind is made up. I cannae let this lad fall between the cracks. He's at that delicate age between child and man, and he, and his mother, need some care. If I walk away from this, I'll never forgive myself.'

She plants her palm in front of my face. 'Stop! You'll get no argument from me. I've just heard Isla's abridged life story, and it's shocked me to my core. Come hell or high water, I'll help them turn it around or die trying—and we need to start right now. You keep an eye on the boys. I'm heading to the supermarket to get some much-needed provisions. I'll restock their cupboards with a few basics but let's order takeaway for tonight. Tomorrow, we'll really get down to business.'

A smile breaks across my face as I lean in and kiss her on the forehead. 'My angel.'

'I'm no angel. I'll tell you that. I'm fucking angry... ropeable! That woman and child have been through hell. She's on her last legs. The abuse, trauma, and belittling are beyond belief—except it's not beyond belief. The only positive out of all this is that their paltry income will not be pissed up against the wall by her drunken, violent husband anymore.' She turns to leave but stops. 'Oh, and the next time I have my head stuck up my arse, can you warn me?'

'Jackie, wait. I have an idea.'

⤜⤛⤜ ⤚⤙⤚

The aluminium trays of Chinese takeaway are scattered around the room. Isla finishes her last mouthful and places her plate on the floor as Scotty picks up another carton of fried rice and tucks in.

'Thank you so much,' Isla begins. 'It's a rare treat when we have a takeaway.'

'Takeaways are nice once in a while,' Jackie says. 'Although, nothing beats home cooking.'

Wallace and Robert lift themselves from the floorboards and collect everyone's plates.

'We'll do the clean up,' Wallace states.

It's a sympathetic gesture, but it will need re-doing once they've finished.

'I'll give you a hand,' Scotty replies as he scoops the last vestiges of rice into his mouth.

The room falls silent. I give Jackie a surreptitious nod.

'Isla, when was the last time you had a holiday?' Jackie says.

Isla appears puzzled for a second. 'Let me see... it was when Scotty was about eighteen months old. We had a long weekend in Scarborough. Yes, that was it because I distinctly remember the weather, which was terrible. It rained for the whole three days.'

'Isla,' I begin, 'the coroner's report, inquest, police investigation is going to take weeks, possibly months.'

'Aye, I suppose it is,' she says as she relaxes back into the threadbare settee.

Jackie takes over the tag team routine. 'How would you like to get away for a week, in a charming old fishing village only three hours' drive from here?'

Isla's eyebrows arch.

'We have a holiday home in Dinkiad Bay. Nothing flash but it is neat and tidy, if a little old fashioned, but cosy, nonetheless. Geordie could drive you and Scotty there tomorrow.'

Isla frowns. 'I'm not sure. I'm afraid I don't have the money for that sort of thing. But thanks for the offer.'

'It will cost you nothing,' I say. 'We barely use it and you'd be doing us a favour by airing the place out. It's a lovely little village with a pub which does meals on a night, a doctor's surgery, a grocery store, and a chippy. The views are to die for. I have fishing tackle in the garden shed so Scotty could cast a line in each day. There're some magnificent walks.'

'Isla,' Jackie says as she rests her hand on top of hers, 'it would do you good. A chance to take stock, grieve, reflect and also a time to plan for the future, yours, and Scotty's future.'

There's a creak from a floorboard. Scotty has been listening from the doorway.

'I think it's a good idea, ma. You really need a break if only to get away from this place.'

'We don't have much money,' Isla retorts.

'I have money. I've saved up everything Geordie paid me over the summer. I have over three hundred quid.'

'And you'll only spend there what you'd spend here anyway,' Jackie offers.

Isla fidgets with the hem of her blouse before breaking out a wistful smile. 'Aye, why not? They say a change is as good as a rest. What time tomorrow?'

'That's the spirit! We'll make an early start. I'll pick you up at seven, sharp. Make sure you're packed. And remember, even though we've had a lovely warm summer—it is Scotland, so pack some woollies. Oh, and while you're away, would you mind if I fixed a few things up around the house?'

'He can be quite a handyman when he puts his mind to it,' Jackie jumps in.

'What sort of things?' Isla replies as though she has become blind to the parlous state of her abode.

'Leaky taps, the front gate, a few broken windows... that sort of thing. Nothing major.'

She shrugs. 'Aye, do what you want with the place, although if I were you, I'd nay bother. The bloody thing needs demolishing.'

I amble down the stairs and into the kitchen, where Jackie is leaning against the bench with a pen in her hand and a notepad on the countertop.

'They're both out like a light,' I say as I pull a beer from the fridge, crack the top and take a hearty slug.

'How were they? Did they mention anything about Scotty and his house?'

'No, not specifically. Wallace asked me why some people are poor, while others are rich. He always asks the hard questions.'

'What did you say?'

'Not much. I mumbled and fumbled my way through codswallop. What are you doing?' I ask as I thirstily pour a beer down my throat.

'I'm making a list of things we need to do. It's going to be tough to get everything done in a week. Do you know if they own the place or are they still renting from the council?'

I drop the empty bottle into the recycle bin.

'According to Scotty, they own it. Isla was left a modest sum when her mother passed away a few years ago and the first thing she did was buy the house outright from the council before the old man could get his hands on the money.'

'Canny woman.'

'Right, I'm away to bed. I'm fair bushed after that traumatic day. Are you coming?'

She pulls a bottle of white wine from the fridge and pours herself a generous glass.

'I'll be up in a while. I've got my thinking cap on, and I want to get as much pre-planning done while I'm in the mood.'

'Okay, I'll see you when you come.'

'Oh, Geordie?'

'What?'

'Did you ring Will and the others?'

'Shit the bed! No... I'll ring him now.' I pull my phone out and prod at his image. 'Hey, Bill, how's things?'

'Good. What's the go?'

'Listen, I need your help for the next week.' I'm greeted with a deep sigh.

'What now?' he asks wearily.

'Remember that lad I was telling you about, Scotty? Well, his dad was killed in an accident about a week ago.'

'I'm sorry to hear that.'

'Don't be. The man was an ogre. Anyway, the lad and his ma are living in squalor. They're really on their uppers and me and Jackie thought we'd give their home a bit of a makeover while they spend a week in the cottage at Dinkiad Bay.'

'Wait, is this the lad who cuts your grass and used to play the guitar?'

'Aye, that's him. We really need all hands on deck.'

'Okay. Count me in. I'll get up there about midday tomorrow.'

'Good. Good man. And one last thing; can you ring Flaky and Robbo and get them to come up as well?'

'Flaky and Robbo!' he says with a certain amount of incredulity. 'I wouldn't trust either to change a lightbulb without blowing up the national grid.'

'They can lift and carry, and push a lawnmower. Even they can't stuff that up.'

'Hmm... famous last words.'

Chapter Twenty-four

The Makeover

I ram the last piece of drive-thru burger into my mouth and wash it down with a glug of tepid bottled water. It's been a whirlwind seven-hour return trip to and from Dinkiad Bay. Isla and Scotty were delighted with the place, and it was warming to see a heavy weight lift from their shoulders when we entered the fishing village.

I park up outside Scotty's house next to a large white transit van hired by Jackie. She appears in the doorway, looking displeased.

'Bloody builder promised to be here by one and it's now gone two.'

I jump from the car and navigate the obstacle course of a garden.

'He's a builder. Of course he's going to be late. It's in their genes,' I reply as I give her a peck on the lips.

'Have you heard from Will and the boys?'

'Yeah, I spoke to Bill twenty minutes ago and told them to come straight here. They should be turning up shortly.'

'Good, because the skip is due to be delivered about now. Let's hope the skip driver is more reliable than the builder.'

The rattle and clanging of a truck has us both peering down the street.

'Speak of the devil. Here comes your builder now.'

The work truck pulls up and a large stocky man with a bushy ginger beard alights.

'Are you Mrs Kincaid?' he queries in a deep but soft, calm tone.

'Aye! And you must be Bob the bloody Builder. You're over an hour late.'

'I'm sorry. I got side-tracked.'

'Have you not got a phone?'

'Yes, but...'

'Never mind all that now! Come on, let's start. We've wasted enough time. I told you on the phone this job was urgent,' Jackie yells as she disappears inside the house.

The builder shuffles past, throwing me a sheepish wince.

'Is that your missus?'

'Yes.'

'Christ. You have my condolences, mate. She has a hell of a tongue on her.'

'Only when riled. A word of advice—don't argue with her. There's only one winner.'

'Thanks. I'll bear that in mind. I'm Gavin Dunbar, by the way.'

'Geordie Kincaid. Pleased to meet you,' I say as we shake hands.

'Mr Dunbar, I'm waiting!' Jackie's voice booms from inside.

I tag along behind as we traipse into the kitchen.

'Okay, now you may wish to take your own notes, but I have everything I want you to do meticulously documented. I'll give you a copy at the end of the walkthrough, but I expect at least a ballpark figure of the costs by seven tonight.'

'I'm not sure I'll be able to...'

Jackie rounds on him. 'Mr Dunbar, you come highly recommended, and this is a mission of mercy for a struggling mother and son who have recently lost their husband and father. They have no money, they can barely feed themselves, they are desperate. Do you not feel beholden to help those less fortunate than yourself?'

'Well... yes, of course, but...'

'No more buts! Good. It's agreed then. You can email me your estimate tonight. Right, let's begin. I want a completely new kitchen. It doesn't have to be state-of-the art, but it must be modern, functional, and easy to clean. There also needs to be an allowance made for a dishwasher, a front loader washing machine, and a tall fridge-freezer.'

Gavin pulls his tape measure from his belt.

'Okay, I'll need to take some measurements.'

'I don't have time for that now,' Jackie barks. 'You can measure up to your heart's content once I've finished with you.'

Gavin raises his eyebrows and expels a long puff of air. I offer him a conciliatory shrug of the shoulders.

'Now follow me,' she continues as she marches out of the kitchen. 'I want new light fittings for every room and new power sockets on every outlet. Don't worry about curtains and rails, or carpets. I'll take care of all that. There are a few broken windows, and some tiles are missing from the roof, so you'll need to check the loft for water damage. Next stop, the bathroom, and toilet.'

Her feet echo around the house as they stamp down hard on the wooden stairs. There's a toot-toot from a car.

'I'll leave you to it, Gavin. Good luck.'

'Thanks, I'm gonna need it,' he replies morosely.

I wander outside as Bill, Flaky, and Robbo emerge from the red Mondeo. I shake my head in disbelief. Billy's attire matches my own. Work boots, old jeans, old shirt. The sort of outfit you wear when you're ready for some hard, dirty work. Flaky is dressed like a trendy accountant and Robbo looks like he's ready for a night out at an upmarket nightclub.

'What are you two wearing?' I shout at them as Robbo sparks up a spliff and surveys the rubbish in the garden. 'Billy Boy, did you not give them the brief?'

'I gave them the brief,' he replies wearily as sticks a smoke into his mouth and rubs the back of his neck.

'I'm here in more of an advisory capacity,' Flaky begins. 'I'm not really a hands-on sort of chap, but every project needs a project manager; and here I am, at your service.'

'I'll second that,' Robbo drawls as he emits a large plume of smoke into the bright sky. 'I'm more of an interior decorator advisor, you know, soft-furnishings, colours, ambience. Think of me as the Giorgio Armani of the north but for houses. I like to take a homeopathic approach to these things.'

'I think you mean holistic,' Flaky corrects.

'Whatevs.'

'Oh no! If you two think you're going to strut around here in your peacock suits offering your unwanted, idiotic advice, then you can think again. You are here for hard work. Anyway, we already have a project manager,' I state emphatically.

Flaky and Robbo appear bemused as they exchange glances.

'Who?' they both question in unison.

'I don't care about your backlog of work, Mr Dunbar!' Jackie's voice rumbles out from the upstairs bathroom window, which is slightly ajar. 'Can you not see this is an emergency? Now you listen to me and listen good...'

Flaky and Robbo stare at me as a flicker of fear ripples across their features.

'Jackie?' Robbo whispers.

'Aye. She's in charge and she's not in the best of moods, so I'd tread lightly if I were you.'

'Will, you said nothing about Jackie being involved in this gig?' Robbo says, patently disturbed by the news.

'Didn't I?' he smirks. 'It must have slipped my mind. Okay Geordie, how about a quick brew while we go through what needs to be done?'

'Aye. Good idea. I'll flick the kettle on.'

⋙⋙ ⋘⋘

'Let me get this right,' Flaky says as he dunks a ginger nut into his cup. 'A new kitchen, bathroom, and toilet. New carpets, white goods, beds, and furniture. A makeover for the gardens—both front and back. Repaint all the walls and ceilings and you and Will are going to build a covered deck and barbecue area?'

'That's what I said,' I reply as I sip on my tea.

'And all in a week?'

'Yep.'

Flaky throws his arms up in the air. 'You're completely delusional. As nutty as a fruit cake. You wouldn't get all that done in two months, never mind a week.'

'And there speaks the prophet of doom, the naysayer. You're always the same.'

'It's rarely I agree with Flaky,' Robbo begins, 'but on this occasion he has a point.'

'What do you think, Bill?' I say, turning to him for support.

He purses his lips together and rubs at the stubble on his chin. 'It would mean early starts and late finishes and meticulous organisation... but yeah, I reckon we could pull it off.'

'Early starts. How early?' Robbo inquires with suspicion.

'Five-thirty out of bed, showered and dressed, breakfast by six. Get to the house by six-thirty and work through until seven, maybe eight at night. Then rinse and repeat for seven days.'

Robbo appears unsteady on his feet as the blood drains from his face.

'Shit the bed...' he murmurs, completely confounded.

A moment's silence is rudely broken as Jackie clomps into the kitchen followed by the harangued builder who appears as befuddled as Robbo.

'Oh, hello boys. I didn't hear you arrive. Ready for the task ahead? I'm guessing Geordie has run you through the itinerary.'

'Yes,' Flaky says. 'It's a tough job, but we'll all put our shoulder to the wheel first thing tomorrow morning.'

Jackie laughs, mockingly. 'Tomorrow? Oh no. You start right now. In the back of the rental van is a lawnmower, strimmer, gloves, and other gardening equipment.'

She's interrupted by a loud bang from outside. 'And that sounds like the skip bin being delivered right now. Perfect timing. Before you knock off tonight, I want all the rubbish from both gardens deposited into the skip and the grass cut and raked up.'

The four of us stare at her with mouths agape. Robbo gives me a sly nod.

'Ahem... sweetheart, me and the boys have been up since the crack of dawn. It's now mid-afternoon. We need a bit of sustenance to gird our loins and maybe indulge in a wee nap. Don't you think it best to make a fresh start first thing tomorrow?'

'No, I bloody well don't! And if it's sustenance you're after... I've already thought of that.'

She pulls open the fridge door. Two shelves are packed with bottles of beer and the third shelf contains an overflowing tray of sandwiches covered in plastic wrap.

'That should keep you going for today.'

'Any water?' Flaky asks nervously.

'Aye. You see that thing over there... above the sink? It's called a tap. You turn it on and, as if by magic, water flows from it. Now grab a drink and a bite to eat... then get to work! Bloody rock stars—weak as piss! Now, Mr Dunbar, where was I?'

'I haven't drunk tap water since I was eighteen,' Flaky moans forlornly.

I pull the tray of sandwiches from the fridge as Bill cracks open three beers and hands them out. Flaky nervously grabs a glass from the cupboard and tiptoes towards the tap as though it's the devil incarnate.

⤛⤜ ⤛⤜

We're four days into the renovation and things are going surprisingly well for a quartet of pampered rock stars who are not used to hard work or manual labour. Two of us are faring okay, and the other two wankers, less so. My heart bleeds for them.

The garden has been cleared of rubbish and the grass cut. We ripped the kitchen and bathroom out yesterday, pulled up the few remnants of carpet and replaced the window coverings. All personal belongings—clothes, pictures, knick-knacks have been removed by Jackie to a storage shed she's rented. Everything else has gone in the skip, which is on its third visit.

It's dusty, dirty, and bloody hot work. We've even fallen into a routine. We arrive on site by six every morning and the first thing we do is have a brew and a smoke as we discuss the agenda for the day, based on Jackie's detailed notes.

At six-thirty prompt we start and work non-stop for three hours, at which point we stop for a morning break which is cooked up on the new barbecue we bought. After another brew, and bacon and egg rolls for three of us, and a veggie burger for Flaky, we crack on again and work for another three hours before stopping for lunch. The routine continues until we've achieved all the tasks for the day, which usually means we knock off between six and seven each night. Then it's back home, a quick shower, and fresh clothes, and downstairs by which time Jackie has a hearty meal waiting for us—and a few cleansing ales.

I've never worked so hard in all my life, but the funny thing is, I'm really enjoying it. To see the house slowly transformed gives me a warm fuzzy feeling inside. I've never slept so well either. Once my head hits the pillow, I'm dead to the world until my alarm wakes me to begin another day.

»»»» ««««

It's mid-morning and unusually warm. I'm holding one end of the tape measure as Bill marks out holes for the supporting posts for the deck and roof.

'Pass me the marker paint,' he says.

I throw him the can and he sprays a large X onto the clay, then adds a rough five inch square around the X.

'Righto, that's the last one. We best head off to the timber yard and get the materials. What are the fuckwit twins up to?'

'I checked on them twenty minutes ago. They've finished repainting Scotty's bedroom and were making a start on the master bedroom. They've got more paint on themselves than on the bloody walls.'

'Who shall we get to dig the holes while we're gone?'

I wince and scratch my head. 'It's a hell of a choice,' I murmur.

'Hmm, you're not wrong, but beggars can't be choosers.'

'I suppose if you held a gun to my head, I'd have to pick Robbo.'

'Really?'

'Aye. He's a dedicated non-thinker. Give him a task to do and he'll do it blindly, like a robotic idiot. Whereas Flaky, well, you know what he's like.'

'Yes, he'll reinvent the wheel. Okay, I'll go tell him.'

I rub a towel across my face and neck, then take a swig of water. The drilling and banging from the builders working in the bathroom momentarily ceases as a heated argument erupts.

'Why me?' Robbo's confused and annoyed voice cries out. 'Why not Flaky?'

'Because he can barely lift a paint brush, never mind dig six holes in hard clay. Anyway, one of you has to do it and I've picked you, so stop your bleating and jump to it. It's all marked out. You need to go down a minimum of 600 mm.'

'Christ! What's that in old money?'

'About two feet.'

'You've got to be fucking joking?'

'I jest ye not. Me and Geordie will be gone a good hour, so you should get at least two or three dug in that time.'

'Isn't there some sort of machine that can do that sort of shit these days?'

'Stop arguing the toss and get on with it. Oh, and Robbo... no slacking, right?'

⠀⠀⠀

We arrive back with all the required timber, fasteners, and rapid set concrete and unload the van. As we dump it in the back garden, Billy inspects the four holes that Robbo has dug.

'Well, well. Miracles can happen,' he says with a smile as he pats a sweating Robbo on the back.

'You know me. Never scared of a bit of hard work,' he replies as he lights a joint.

The smile slowly fades from Bill's face as he takes a closer inspection of the holes. He grabs the tape measure and places the end against the brickwork of the house and extracts the tape.

'I don't believe it,' he whispers with an air of desperation.

'What is it?' I ask.

'He's moved the bloody holes by about four inches.'

'What's wrong with that?' Robbo says. 'The ground was too hard where you had it originally marked out. What's a few inches between friends?' he laughs nervously.

'You useless numpty!' I roar. 'All the timber has been cut to size!'

Robbo nervously scratches his stubble. 'What does that mean?'

'It means all the joists and decking timber will be four inches short.'

There's a worrying squeal from upstairs, followed by the tinkle of glass and a dull thud from the front of the house. We stare at each other in silence before Flaky pokes his head out from an upstairs window.

'Erm, slight accident, chaps.'

Billy closes his eyes. 'Go on,' he says jadedly.

'I knocked the paint tin off the trestle boards, and it fell through the window and onto the front path.'

'How much?'

'A full tin... a big one, and ahem, open. Oh, and it broke the window.'

'Christ! More spot fires to put out,' I curse. 'Shift your sorry arse and get the hose pipe on it now.'

Chapter Twenty-five

Charitable Donations

It's early evening as we slump into four camp chairs. Robbo passes the plate of sandwiches along, as Billy hands out the beer.

'She makes a mean sandwich, your missus,' Robbo mumbles through a mouthful of egg and cress.

With a welcoming glug of beer, I relax back and admire our handiwork. All the posts, joists, and decking have been erected.

'We'll put the roof on first thing tomorrow,' Billy says. 'Then Robbo can stain the timber.'

'Yoo-hoo! Only me,' Jackie calls out.

She saunters into the back garden and eyes us suspiciously.

'It's funny that every time I call around, you lot are filling your faces and swilling beer.'

'Purely coincidental,' Robbo says.

She becomes distracted as her eyes fall on the deck.

'My oh my! That looks brilliant! Well done, boys. You have been working hard.' Her enthusiasm doesn't last long. 'Has the roofer been?'

'Yes, my love, all done. And the plumber has been. Kitchen and bathroom are finished. The tiler arrives tomorrow to do the splashbacks.'

'It's going to be very busy tomorrow. The carpet layers are also arriving, so keep out of their way. Will, did you order the trees, shrubs, and plants from the nursery?'

'Yes. Arriving Saturday morning. I'll get Robbo to dig the holes tomorrow.'

'Good. Oh, I must buy a small table and chairs for the deck, and Geordie?'

'Yes, my love?'

'Have you got those things for Scotty's bedroom?'

'Aye. They're at home. I'll bring them down on Monday.'

'Don't leave it too late. I'm planning on picking Scotty and Isla up mid-morning, so we should be back here by one. You haven't forgotten about the barbecue, have you?'

'No, dear.'

'Make sure you give it a good scrub down. I want it looking like new. Right, I'm going to head back home to prepare an evening meal. How long will you lot be?'

'About an hour. We're about finished for the day. Just got to have a bit of a clean up.'

'Good. Right, I'll see you back there.'

We exchange glances with one another as she marches away.

'There's a woman on a mission,' Flaky comments.

'Hell's bells, Geordie, how much is this lot costing you?' Robbo drawls as he stuffs another sandwich into his mouth.

'Last count… nudging forty grand. I dare say there'll be another five grand before we're done.'

'That's no small amount of bread.'

'Geordie won't be paying it all,' Billy states.

I exchange glances with Robbo and Flaky.

'And who will pay for it?' Flaky says with a creased brow.

'All of us.'

'And who made this decision?'

'I did. Do you disagree?'

Flaky and Robbo fidget uncomfortably. 'I'm not saying I agree or disagree, but it would have been nice to have been consulted about it. You know how the band works.'

I sense an imminent flare up. 'That's a generous offer, Billy Boy, but I wouldnae hear of it. This is my project and me and Jackie will bear the costs.'

Bill swigs down the last of his beer and cracks another. 'Thirsty work, this building lark. How many charity gigs have we done over the years? Thirty, forty?'

'More like sixty,' Robbo says as he follows Bill's lead and helps himself to a fresh bottle.

'We do the gig, and the money is transferred to the charity, and that's the last we hear of it. Who knows where it actually goes? I know for a fact that for every pound raised, only a percentage gets through to the actual people needing it.'

'Charities have running costs the same as any other business,' Flaky states.

'True. And some have higher running costs than others due to CEO's swanning around in luxury cars and getting fat at flash restaurants on their expense accounts. No, this is different. It feels good to not only pay for everything, but to get our hands dirty for a change. This is a band effort. We're a team. Anyway, we have that other charity gig coming up in four weeks. The money we make from merchandise alone will cover the cost of this reno. Are we all agreed?'

'Aye, fair enough,' Robbo says.

'Yes, I'm sorry. You're right,' Flaky murmurs.

'Good. Right, let's tidy up. One last push for the day.'

We rise wearily to our feet as I pat Bill on the back.

'Cheers Bill, you're a good man,' I say.

'Am I?' he replies cryptically.

⤐⥤⥤⥤ ⥢⥢⥢⥢⟵

Seven days have passed since I dropped Scotty and his mother at Dinkiad Bay. We're at their house putting the final finishing touches to everything as Jackie strides around like a sergeant major barking orders at everyone.

'Robbo, the back, and front lawn could do with a quick mow. The grass is getting a tad long for my liking.'

'Yes, Jackie,' he replies.

'And Geordie, Will, when's the garden shed arriving?'

'Any moment now, sweetpea.'

'Are you and Will going to get it up in time?'

'Never fear, Jackie,' Billy says with a lascivious smile. 'Me and Geordie are the masters of fast erections.'

She throws him a disapproving glance. 'Is that right?' she says in a low growl. 'Let's hope it's not a disappointment like so many erections are. We don't want it coming down before it's fulfilled its job.'

Bill smiles at me. 'She's a killer.'

'Tell me about it.'

'I hope you've got a sturdy lock on it. The crime rate around here is horrendous,' she continues unabated.

'Jackie, my love. It's a wooden garden shed, pre-made. If someone really wants to break into it... they will. We have security lights and cameras installed as a deterrent.'

'My neighbour had his security cameras stolen,' Robbo adds, unhelpfully, as he unfurls the power lead to the lawnmower.

'Cheeky bastards.'

Jackie checks her watch, agitated and impatient. 'Okay, I should be back around two. Geordie, I'll call you thirty minutes before I arrive. Mam will bring Robert and Wallace over at some point. I want you to greet Scotty and Isla as they get out of the car. The rest of you stay in the back garden and crank the barbecue. Where's Flaky?' she asks, scanning the back garden.

'Call of nature,' I say.

She pulls a disgusted frown, as though visiting the toilet is dirty.

'Oh, and one last thing—keep off the pop until this afternoon. Do I make myself clear?'

'Yes, Jackie,' we reply in reluctant agreement.

'You make us sound like raging alcoholics. You know, it can knock a man's confidence to be forever harangued based on one or two past deeds,' I implore.

Her eyes narrow. 'You three have history—a long history.' There's an eyeball-to-eyeball Mexican standoff for a moment before she snaps from her suspicions. 'Good. Right, well hop to it! I want everything looking tip top and tickety-boo by the time I arrive back. Bye!'

We stand in silence until we hear the roar of the Range Rover start up and move off. We give it another few seconds to be on the safe side. I turn to Bill and Robbo.

'I suggest a quick beer, and smoke before we really bend our backs?'

They both crack a smile. 'Now you're talking,' Robbo says. 'Only the one, though.'

'Aye. Only the one. Everything in moderation—it's my middle name.'

There's a rush of water down the pipe from the toilet and a few seconds later, Flaky appears. He gawps open-mouthed at us before checking his watch.

'I swear to God you lot are getting worse! It's barely turned ten o'clock!'

'Oh, stop your quibbling, you big Jesse, and either grab a beer or keep your big cake hole shut! We've earned this.'

⇢⇢⇢ ⇠⇠⇠

I'm putting the finishing touches to Scotty's bedroom as Bill walks in.

'What do you think, Bill?'

'Compact and bijou, but everything a teenage lad needs. A comfy bed, a new laptop, small desk, and chair, and best of all, a sound system.'

'Aye. State-of-the art. Plays MP3s, CDs, connects to the internet, and best of all it has a record player. I went down to the second-hand shop in the market and got some classics very cheaply.'

I pull out the LPs and hand them to Bill as I read them out.

'BB King, Big Bill Broonzy, The Faces, Rod Stewart, Muddy Waters, The Stones, The Who, The Beatles, Kinks.'

'Nice selection.'

My phone rings. 'Hi, Geordie, it's me, Jackie.'

'Yes, love, I know it's you. I have a special ringtone and your face pops up when you call.'

'I'm twenty minutes away. Now remember, meet me outside and we'll do the walkthrough together. And tell Will to fire up the barbecue and pull the meat out of the fridge to come to room temperature.'

'Yes, sweetheart.'

'Did you get everything done? No disasters?'

'Of course we did. And no disasters.'

'Has someone cleaned the toilet?'

'What toilet?'

'What do you mean, what toilet?'

I pull the phone away from my ear and shake my head.

'It was a joke, sweetheart. I'll get Robbo to check in a moment.'

'Good. Love you and see you soon. I'm so excited. They've no idea. You won't believe the change in their appearance after a week away from it all. They're like new people.'

'That's nice. See you soon.'

Chapter Twenty-six

Paying It Forward

I open the door to the Range Rover as Scotty spills out and gives me a big, unexpected hug.

'Geordie, what a brilliant place Dinkiad Bay is. I got up early every morning, about sixish, and wandered along the beach and did a spot of fishing. I caught a couple of mackerel and some old guy taught me how to fillet and cook them. Fresh as. I've never had fish before, not unless it's covered in batter. Then, I found an old guitar of yours... I think it was a Spanish guitar, wide fretboard. I hope you don't mind. It took a couple of days until the pads of my fingers had grown another skin, then I couldn't stop playing it. Everything came back.'

Isla steps from the car and gives me a peck on the cheek.

'The young tyke was obsessed with the damn thing. Spent most of his time in the bedroom practising.'

'That's not true ma! We had our daily walk together, our evening meal at the pub, and a game of scrabble on a night.'

Isla strokes her son's cheek. 'I'm only messing with you, son. I enjoyed every minute.'

Her attention is diverted to the front garden. 'Oh my, I cannae believe it! Look how neat and tidy it looks. And a new fence and gate. My God, we can now see the garden path.'

'Come on Isla, Scotty, let me and Geordie show you around inside.'

As we enter the house Scotty becomes mute whilst Isla gushes at every improvement. As we enter the kitchen, she wobbles, and drops to her knees. Jackie rushes to her aid.

'Are you all right Isla? Do you not like it?' Jackie throws me a worrying glance.

Maybe we've overdone it. After all, it was their home and with no input from them, we've gutted it and started again. Have we thrown out the memories with the bathwater? Jackie pulls Isla to her feet.

'I'm sorry Jackie, I really am. I don't know what to say.'

'Do you like it or not? Have we gone too far?'

A tear streaks her cheek as she sniffles. 'No. I love it. But I can never pay you back. We cannae afford this.'

Jackie grabs her by the shoulders and pulls her into her bosom. 'Oh, Isla! You don't have to pay us back. It's our gift. Actually, I'll rephrase that: you do have to pay us back.'

Everyone freezes before Jackie sprouts a broad beam.

'The payback is that you and Scotty have a fresh start. Don't waste it. Grab it with both hands and tell yourself you deserve a better life. That's the payback. What we've done is lay the first building block. The rest is up to you and Scotty.'

As Isla bursts into tears and nuzzles into Jackie's shoulder, I lead Scotty out of the kitchen and up the stairs.

'We'll look at your bedroom,' I whisper.

The boy is still mute and I'm still not sure if he approves or not. I'm feeling like an interfering neighbour who means well but is a royal pain in the arse. As we saunter into his bedroom, he stops dead in his tracks as his eyes work overtime, taking in the new surroundings.

'What do you think?' I ask nervously.

There's silence before he turns to me. I stare into his eyes and notice something has changed. Where I used to see fear, lack of confidence, and hesitation, now I see resolve... and a fire.

'Why?' he asks.

'Why not?'

'I'm being serious.'

I sigh and sit down on the bed. He drops alongside me, clasps his hands together, and stares at his well-worn trainers, which are falling apart.

'Okay, I'll be serious for a moment. Remember I told you the story of how the band formed, how we split up and how I fell on hard times. Then Bill turned up one day and suggested the reunion tour?'

'Yes. What of it?'

'I said the rest was history, but it wasn't. I lied.'

'I don't understand?'

'When Bill proposed the tour, I declined.'

'Why?'

'I was scared of my own shadow. I'd lost my confidence.'

'You?' he says, astounded at the revelation.

'Aye. Me, the big hard man, Geordie Kincaid. But Bill still believed in me. After much soul searching and a few arguments, he convinced me to join the tour. I loved it! It was like putting on an old pair of slippers—except, towards the end of the tour, my Nan passed away.

I was bereft, heartbroken. She was my surrogate mother. The day after my Nan died, I met Jackie, and she has been the making of me. She's a hard taskmaster, but that's what I needed. All up, Billy sort of saved me twice. My Nan saved me twice and Jackie is my last saviour.'

The boy falls silent again with a confused look as he fidgets with the bottom of his shirt.

'I think I get it,' he starts tentatively. 'That time in your kitchen when you spoke about passing it forward... is this what you're doing?'

'Correct.'

'But why me?'

'Pure chance. I took my lads to the park. You sat down on the bench next to me and I knew you were at a crossroads and needed help.'

'It could have been anyone?'

'I guess so. That's what chance is. As Billy Boy likes to say when he's writing songs, if it comes a knocking on your door, make sure you open it.'

The lad smiles and stands up. 'Thanks Geordie! I get it now.'

'One day it will be your turn to pay it forward... don't forget that.'

'I won't.'

'Knock, knock,' Bill's voice calls out as he enters the room. 'Not interrupting, am I?'

'Nah, all done,' I say, rising from the bed.

Scotty is now in an excited state of agitation as he marvels at his new laptop, sound system, and vinyl records.

'Hey, Scotty,' Bill says quietly. 'Look under your bed.'

The lad turns to him, appearing bemused before crouching to his knees and sliding his hand under the bed. He grabs at something and pulls it out. I'm as surprised as he is. He lays the guitar case on his bed and undoes the clasps. An acoustic guitar stares back up at him. It was the first guitar Billy bought once he'd come into some money, many moons ago.

'Is it for me?' the lad stammers.

'Yep. Yours to keep. I wrote four number ones on that little beauty, plus two early albums. Geordie tells me you're keen on music and play guitar. I thought this would get you off on the right track.'

It's a hell of a gift. An original Gibson Hummingbird would come with a hefty price tag. Add to that, the fact Billy wrote four number ones with it, then it becomes priceless. Bill pulls a beaten-up old guitar strap from the case.

'And this is yours, too. Black Buffalo hide. It's been around the world four times and seen some things.'

'Thankfully, guitar straps can't talk,' I add.

The lad tentatively attaches the strap to the guitar, slings it over his shoulders and plays a few gentle, open chords.

'It's brill!' he exclaims. 'The action is amazing. It's like playing cotton strings.'

Billy smiles proudly. 'Never goes out of tune. Best guitar I ever owned, but it's time for it to have a new owner. The next generation. Don't waste it.'

'Rest assured, I won't.'

I pick up a sense of something deeper going on in Bill's words.

'Come on then,' I say. 'You reckon you've been banging away on my rusty old Spanish guitar in Dinkiad Bay... let's hear what you've got.'

The lad's embarrassed.

'Okay, but I only have two songs that are completely finished. The others are works in progress.'

'Fire away,' I reply as I sit back down on the bed as Bill joins me.

To be honest, I'm not expecting much from a broken kid who used to play guitar until his dad pawned it.

Scotty girds himself, then begins.

It's a robust, punky intro, which I'm mightily impressed with. Bill shoots me a confused sideways glance. The lad launches into the verse and chorus. The performance is incongruous to his narrow frame and gaunt appearance. He can not only play the guitar but has all the vocal skills of a veteran rock star. His lyrics hit the solar plexus; pithily dry, sarcastic, salient, and foreshadowing possible future events.

He immediately goes into the second song, as good as the first. As he finishes, he appears rather sheepish, as if he's made a fool of himself. He stares at the new carpet, then drops the neck of the guitar towards the floor. He's even looking like a tortured rock star.

'What do you think, Bill?' I ask, knowing the answer

'Not bad. In fact, very good. All the makings of a songwriter and performer.'

'I have to concur. A couple of good 'uns.'

Scotty lifts his head and stares at us. 'You're just saying that,' he accuses sullenly.

Billy Boy laughs. 'You don't know me and Geordie very well. When it comes to music, if we don't like something, we'll let you know.'

'Although,' I say as I throw a glance at Bill. 'They could be improved.'

'True. Let's do it now. Ten minutes fine tuning and you'll have a couple of crackers. You up for that, Scotty?' Billy says with an excited grin.

'Am I ever!'

⋙ ⋘

We are in the back garden enjoying the barbecue as the sun heads to its resting place for the night. As I suck on a beer, Billy pulls me to one side.

'Geordie, a quiet word. I'll meet you in the shed in two minutes, right?'

'Aye, okay.' I'm puzzled and a little concerned about his request.

I slip away without being noticed. Inside, Bill is relaxing in a camp chair surrounded by various gardening paraphernalia. There's barely room for me to stand up. He's been acting strange for at least eighteen months, and without directly confronting him with it, I think I know why.

'What's the go?' I ask.

'The charity gig in four weeks' time.'

I scratch under my chin. It's not what I was expecting, but it's still not good.

'Billy Boy, we have TV and radio all lined up. It's syndicated across the globe. About thirty thousand are expected. The sound crew, the roadies, support bands, the catering — everything is organised. The three charities will make hundreds of thousands. You cannae pull the plug at this late stage.'

He pulls out a smoke and sparks up. The tiny space fills with blue smoke. He appears troubled.

'Geordie, what the hell are you wittering on about? I've no intention of pulling the gig.'

Relief washes through me, but I'm still nervous. 'Okay... well then, what is it?'

Chapter Twenty-seven

Grand Finale – Will's Advice

Geordie is now on stage after The Green Circles delivered a brilliant performance, warming the crowd up nicely. I'm watching from the wings as Geordie grabs the microphone. The crowd go absolutely nuts chanting his name.

'Okay, okay, calm down,' he implores, moving his hand up and down.

His words have no effect as the throng surge forward, throwing their arms in the air, chanting his name.

"Geordie! Geordie! Geordie!"

'What do you reckon the numbers are?' Robbo drawls as he takes a seat at the side of me and Flaky in the wings, and tokes on a spliff.

'Not sure. But it's well over the estimated thirty thousand. I think we may end up getting a lecture from the Chief Constable after this.'

'Aye, well, the weather has been fantastic, for Scotland, and who can resist a free open-air concert?'

'If you're not going to shut up, then I'm going home!' Geordie bellows into the mic.

The assembled multitude slowly quietens.

'Thank you, that's better. I cannae hear myself think up here. Where do you lot think you are—a football match?'

'Offside, referee!' some wag bellows.

'Oh, hilarious, a comedian, eh? Right, I want to be serious for a moment. This may be a free gig, but we're here to raise funds and awareness for several charities, namely Save the Children, NSPCC, and the Refuge Against Domestic Violence. I ask each one of you to get on your phones either now or later and ring the number on the screen behind me. An operator will answer your call, ask for your credit card details and how much you want to donate. I've already been reliably informed that so far, we have raised a paltry half million. Frankly, it's not good enough. Now stop being fucking tight arses and get your credit cards out!'

'Great,' Flaky murmurs. 'The concert is being televised live into thirty countries and Geordie drops the F bomb. You should have gone out there, Will.'

I shake my head. 'No. This is Geordie's hometown, and this gig is his baby. Anyway, what does one swear word matter when it may galvanise people to put their hands in their pockets?'

Flaky and Robbo wander off as Scotty slopes towards me, clutching his guitar. His face is wan, and he keeps swallowing hard. I put my arm around his shoulder.

'How, how long before I'm on?' he asks, terrified.

'Any moment now. Once the great orator has finished threatening the audience.'

He tries to smile but can't.

'How are you feeling?'

'I'm shitting bricks. I'm not sure I can do it, Will. Is it too late to back out? No one even knows I'm playing.'

'No, it's not too late. What you're experiencing is perfectly natural. Don't think of it as fear. Imagine it's excitement. It will give you an edge. Geordie tells me you've been putting in a lot of practice.'

'Yes, he's been pushing me hard. Five hours a day, every day for the past month. I can honestly say I'm beginning to hate those two songs.'

I chuckle. 'You'll fall in love with them again once you get this gig under your belt.'

Geordie finishes haranguing the audience. 'Right, before The Shooting Tsars take to the stage, I have a little surprise for you all,' he yells, revving the crowd up.

The audience responds with a collective, "ooh!"

'I thought you'd like that. Do you want to know what it is?'

"Yes, please, Geordie!" the horde slowly yells, as if they're at a pantomime.

'We have a young lad making his debut tonight. He's only playing the two songs.'

A collective boo resonates around the park.

Geordie stalks the stage as he eyes the audience suspiciously.

'What was that you said?' he says, putting his hand to his ear.

The crowd responds with another boo.

'Aye, I thought that's what you said. You're testing my patience now. Unless you start being nice, then you can all go to your rooms for an hour to think about your actions.'

'A-w-w-w!' the audience responds.

'I thought that might work. Now, are you going to be nice?'

"Yes, Geordie!"

'Good, that's better! Manners cost nothing.'

'How does he do it?' Scotty murmurs as the first smile of the day flashes across his face.

'Some people are born with it,' I reply.

Geordie continues. 'This young Edinburgh lad has only recently turned sixteen, and this is his very first live performance. Remember where you saw him first, as he's a future superstar. Now put your hands together for Scotty Rafferty!'

The gathering erupts into deafening cheers. The sound travels like a tsunami and crashes onto the stage. The hairs on the back of my neck respond as if I've been zapped with a lightning bolt. I pat Scotty on the shoulder.

'Feel that energy—it's yours to feed off,' I say to Scotty, who is in danger of self-combusting.

I'll try a different tack. 'Do you know why people come to concerts?'

'To listen to music?'

'They can listen to music anywhere, anytime, anyhow. No, they come to pay homage to someone who is like them but isn't them. Someone who has broken free of the shackles. They don't come to watch someone who is cowed by life, they can get that anywhere. They want heroes. Now, be a fucking hero, just for one day. In eight minutes, your life will have changed forever. Stroll onto that stage as though you're the coolest rock 'n' roll star in the world. '

He takes a deep breath, swings his acoustic guitar around his back, straightens to his full height and strides onto the stage as the crowd chant his name.

"Scotty, Scotty, Scotty."

'Remember to breathe!' I yell. I don't think he heard me.

Geordie meets him half-way as they exchange fist bumps. He quickly plugs in his guitar and rips into his first song, the up-tempo, punky number with a brilliant chorus and verse.

Geordie joins me in the wings. 'How is he?'

'Nervous, as to be expected. But he's going to be all right. Look at him go, he's like a seasoned pro already.'

'We'll need to watch out for him. The vultures will be circling after this performance.'

I sigh. 'Yep, I know. We'll take him under our wing until he's learnt the ropes. Right, I better do some vocal warmups. I'll see you on stage in twenty.'

'Aye. Let's make it a bloody good one, Billy Boy.'

'Do we know any other way?' I say as I head towards the dressing room.

'No, Bill, we don't. And long may it continue,' he calls out.

'But not too long, eh? We don't want to pass our expiry date and outstay our welcome... do we?'

Thank You

I hope you enjoyed **What's It All About, Geordie?** from my **Shooting Star** series.

If you've missed any of the books in the series, there's a reading order below, although, each book can be read as a standalone.

Let Us Keep In Touch

If you wish to keep up to date with my book news, there are a few simple ways to be notified. You can subscribe to my entertaining (subjective) monthly "**Discombobulated**" newsletter. This not only keeps you abreast of new releases, but occasionally I have a free book to giveaway or promotional discounts. The newsletter is designed to entertain. There's no hard sell and I won't be inundating you with spammy "buy, buy, buy" nonsense – which I personally detest. You can sign up by following the link below, which will take you to my website.

I would like to subscribe to your newsletter.

Alternatively, you can go to the following sites and click on the "**Follow**" button.

BookBub Amazon Facebook

For paperback readers, the links above won't work no matter how many times you tap your finger on the paper. Below is a manual link to type into your browser.

https://www.subscribepage.com/author_simon_northouse_home

If you enjoyed this book, then *reviews* are greatly appreciated. If you wish to contact me, my email address is: **simon@simonnorthouse.com** I enjoy a friendly chat, and will always reply.

Also By Simon Northouse

The Shooting Star Series
Arc Of A Shooting Star (Novel)
The Resurrection Tour Diaries (Short Story)
Catch A Shooting Star (Novel)
Fall Of A Shooting Star (Novel)
What's It All About... Geordie? (Novel)
Nuts At Christmas (Novella)
Eggs Unscrambled (Novel)
I Will Survive (Novel)

Bells At Christmas (Novel)
Tuscan Run (Novel) Pre-Order - Out July 2022

The Soul Love Series
Soul Love (Prequel Novella)
Love Is The Goal (Novel)
Love On A Roll (Novel)
Love Of The Coal (Novel) - 2022/23

The Discombobulated Newsletter Series
Keep On Keeping On (Novella)
Keep Karma and Carry On (Novella)
The Lockdown Diary Blues (Novella)
Carry On Rewardless (Novella)
Keeping On Again! 4 Book Boxset/Omnibus Edition (Novel)

Printed in Great Britain
by Amazon

80203694R00140